39749

Stepfamily

Stepfamily

By
ANNE EMERY

THE WESTMINSTER PRESS
Philadelphia

BOOK DESIGN BY DOROTHY ALDEN SMITH

First edition

PUBLISHED BY THE WESTMINSTER PRESS®
PHILADELPHIA, PENNSYLVANIA

PRINTED IN THE UNITED STATES OF AMERICA

9 8 7 6 5 4 3 2 1

Library of Congress Cataloging in Publication Data

Emery, Anne, 1907–
  Stepfamily.

  SUMMARY: A year and a half after her mother dies, Liza finds her life further complicated when her father remarries and she has a stepbrother she adores and a stepsister she hates.
  [1. Remarriage—Fiction]   I. Title.
PZ7.E587St   [Fic]   79-26908
ISBN 0-664-32660-9

Stepfamily

1

"I'D FEEL A LOT BETTER about the whole thing if I could just like Jennie Duncan," Liza Mackay said ominously, staring at the copper teakettle on the range. It needed polishing. "I mean, she's going to be a stepsister, and I can't stand her!"

Why should she polish a copper kettle for somebody she didn't even like? She knew she would get no sympathy from her brother Matt. He was a year and a half older, and he thought Jennie was beautiful.

The trouble was, she was—blond and slim and lovely. And melancholy in a mysterious way. Not saying much, not smiling often. She made Liza feel like a clod—dark, fat, dowdy, weighing a hundred and sixty pounds, and a freshman in a new high school next month. The thought overwhelmed Liza with misery. She got up from the table and plucked six ginger cookies from the apple-shaped cookie jar.

"Oh, for the lova Pete!" Matt exploded, slamming his soda can down on the table so Coke spattered out the top. "You're complaining all the time about being fat, and all you do is eat!"

He scowled and drank some more Coke. He was

dark like his sister, but string-bean tall and thin, with brown eyes that looked troubled a lot of the time, about all the things he found no answers for.

"You're just a food addict," he told his sister.

"Don't knock it," she retorted. "Eating's better than smoking, I guess."

She ate another ginger cookie, and Matt got up and fetched a handful for himself. Mr. Judge, the basset hound and family clown, sat up beside Liza, looking at her prayerfully. She gave him a cookie and laughed at him. Mr. Judge could always pull her out of a fit of melancholy.

"After all, I baked these cookies," she reminded Matt. "If you want me to give up food, I'll give up cooking too. Okay?"

Liza was a very good cook. She baked bread, cookies, cakes, and rolls which the family loved. And if she didn't, who would? Liza had been the cook for the Mackay family since they had lost Mom a year and a half ago.

Mom had always kept that kettle polished, she remembered. But the kitchen had been Liza's ever since she was twelve and a half. The other kids came and went through the kitchen, getting milk, eating snacks, making sandwiches, and clamoring for Liza's goodies.

She got up from her chair and looked at herself in the long mirror on the door leading to the back stairway, standing sideways and pulling in her stomach, holding her breath, smoothing down her sleeveless dress . . . she didn't look so bad. In fact she looked a little thinner today, and she had two more weeks before school started. All she had to do was—well—wish a little harder.

"Why don't you like Jennie?" Matt asked. "I thought you liked everyone, Liza. And Jennie is a real good kid."

"Sure she is!" Liza snapped. "And you don't like Steve. So who's talking?"

"But that's different!"

Liza lifted her chin. "It's not different at all. For my money, Steve's a lot nicer than his sister."

Matt grinned as if he had been given an unexpected weapon. "Aha! So you like Steve! What makes you think he'd look at someone who weighs a hundred and sixty pounds?"

It was an unexpected blow from Matt, and without warning, Liza felt tears well up and overflow. "I absolutely hate you, Matt Mackay!" she screamed. "Keep out of my way or I'll kill you sometime if you talk to me like that!"

"Well, like I said, just quit eating."

The worst of it was the sinking feeling that Matt was changing, that she was changing, that neither of them was as nice as they used to be. And she knew exactly why they were both edgy right now. Today their father was returning from his ten-day honeymoon with his new wife, Maggie Duncan. And Maggie's three children would join the four Mackay children to become one big family—forever, Liza thought despondently.

Maggie was nice. Liza knew that. Dad had been lonely. He needed Maggie very much. And all his children had told him to go ahead, she would be

11

great, they would all love her.

So why was Liza being so ugly today? She glanced around for the Sunday paper and found it on the floor under the table. Looking up the horoscope for the day, she found her own sign and read: "Agitation will not solve your problems. Make an effort to break with the past. If you participate enthusiastically in a new challenge facing you, you can achieve much."

She dropped the paper, awestruck at the truth the stars revealed, just as the front door opened and Dad cried, "We're home, kids! Where are you all?"

Liza mopped her eyes and rushed to be the first to hug her dad.

Then she looked at Maggie, who was smiling as if she was really glad to see Liza, and Liza felt awkward with her hands, not knowing quite what to do with them. Trying to smile brightly, she said, "Maggie, it's nice to have you home." But could not bring herself to shake hands—that didn't seem exactly right with a brand-new stepmother. But she wasn't ready for hugging and kissing yet. So she hung back, feeling uncertain and hoping her father wasn't disappointed in her, watching Matt.

He cried, "Hi, Dad! Gee, it's great to have you home!" And then he looked at Maggie and said, "We're real glad to have you, Maggie!" And Maggie broke into a quick, warm smile and said, "That's good to hear, Matt!"

Liza thought Matt always knew how to act. Maybe she should have been more enthusiastic. But should you act a lot more loving than you really feel?

She told herself she could not be a hypocrite. But Dad had told her before that acting friendly was not being hypocritical, so now she just felt awkward and looked around again for the younger kids. Ten-year-old Andy came racing downstairs and flung himself into Maggie's arms, and Liza realized sharply that Andy had suffered from his mother's death perhaps deeper and longer than anyone. He had attached himself to Maggie from the beginning. Eight-year-old Becky came down, smiling shyly, to be hugged and kissed. And Gram came in from her bedroom to welcome her son and new daughter-in-law.

"The kids have been wonderful while you were away," she said, kissing both of them. "I'm amazed at how competent Liza is." She smiled at Liza and put her arm around her, and Liza leaned her head on Gram's shoulder and felt comforted.

Then Maggie and Don went on to pick up Maggie's children, and Liza said, "I guess I'll polish that kettle before I get dressed." After that she went upstairs to fix her hair and try to look as beautiful as possible—which was a laugh—before Steve walked in with his mother. Liza wanted to be alone in this last hour before they were all together for keeps, and she thought once more about the shattering changes the Mackays had lived through in the past year and a half.

The shock of her mother's death. . . . They were living in Seattle, then, and Mom had gone shopping one day in March, over a year ago, and was killed in a crash on the highway when another car swung into hers. As simple as that. Liza held herself tight, remembering. Besides grieving for Mom and missing her painfully, she had felt every day for months as if she might lose any of her family as unexpectedly as she had lost Mom, as if she herself could be killed any hour without warning. That terror was a side of mourning no one had ever told her about, and it was added pain.

Gram had come up from Los Angeles, where she was the president of a real estate firm, to help the family get organized again. She showed Liza about the washing machine and dryer, about cooking and taking care of the kitchen.

Liza liked cooking. It was something to take her mind off grief, something she was good at, and the rest of the family loved the results. She made cookies and cakes and ate them for comfort. That was when she began to gain weight.

Right after that Christmas, when everyone missed Mom even more than earlier, Dad lost his job. He was a research engineer at Boeing, and he was laid off with twenty other engineers in January.

"I can do some of the housework while you're in school," he told Matt and Liza, talking about this new disaster. "I'll be home quite a lot until something turns up. It shouldn't take too long . . ."

But nothing did turn up, and after the first few weeks no one asked about it. Dad was worried and silent a lot of the time, and the kids worried with him. Sometime later Liza realized that when they were concerned with Dad's troubles the grief for Mom began to fade a little.

14

In April, Dad asked Gram to come up and stay with the kids again while he went to a small town some ninety miles north of Seattle to see about a job. He had called an old army friend, Howie, who had a repair and appliance shop in Avalon, and Howie said he could use another repairman, if Dad wanted to come and see him about it.

"He says he's got more calls than he can take," Dad told Gram over the telephone the day after he reached Avalon. "It means going out on house calls, the pay is good, and it'll be great working with old Howie. He hasn't changed a bit! And living here is cheaper than in Seattle. I'm starting tomorrow. Can you take care of selling the house there? The kids can come up here as soon as school is out."

So Gram stayed through the last weeks of school, packing and cleaning and getting the family organized to move to Avalon as soon as school was out in June.

Sometimes Liza could not believe they were leaving the house where she had lived as long as she could remember. It was going to hurt later. But for those weeks she was so busy about what to take and what to leave, and with the last visits and farewells with friends, that she had no time to think about not being able to see old friends anymore.

The house was sold . . . she felt cut loose and drifting . . . she was leaving next month . . . next week . . .

Dad came back to Seattle on Memorial Day weekend to take the boat, *Tinker Bell,* to Avalon, and the next Saturday he would return to move the family, and Gram could go back to Los Angeles and her job.

Liza took a last walk around the garden her mother had worked over with love and energy, looking at the flowers her mother had delighted in. The yellow rose was in full bloom. The lavender scented the air as she approached the entrance to the house. The madrona that curved up over the roof carried small white flowers, but when they turned into red berries in the fall, Liza would not see them this year. She was numb with the effort of change, and now she hoped the numbness would last until—well, until she got used to the other place.

2

THE MACKAYS drove up to Avalon early in June, in the station wagon which was stuffed with clothes and sleeping bags and all the belongings that hadn't gone with the moving van. Dad was exhilarated about the move. He kept talking about a different life in the new town and saying wait till they saw the place he had found for them to live in. He was a different man, relaxed, brown, and happy, since he had left Seattle six weeks ago. Liza noticed the change, pleased and puzzled. How had it happened so fast?

He pulled up in front of an old Victorian frame building that looked to Liza's disbelieving eyes as if it were going to fall apart in the next high wind, and jumped out of the car with the most excitement she had ever seen him show.

"You wouldn't believe how lucky I was to find this place!" he said joyously. "It was a small hotel once, and it's been closed down, sitting in probate, nobody paying any attention to it . . . the realtor was amazed when I wanted to buy it. For a third of what we got for the Seattle house! We can fix it up so we'll be living comfortably by the end of summer. There'll be plenty of work for everyone."

The clapboard structure was three stories high, with a veranda sagging around two sides, its roof propped up at one corner on a piece of rusting pipe. Elaborate gingerbread carving clung to the corners of the other supports, looking like tattered shreds where paint was peeling and bits were broken out. The building stood almost alone in a short block, where the only other structure was an empty store at the far corner.

And the old stone building across the street was no prize either.

Incredulous, Liza looked at the overgrown weeds around the shaky steps up to the veranda and the two rusting old cars abandoned in the side yard. She had never seen such a crummy place in her life. And Dad talked about living here?

"We'll have lots of space for a garden!" Dad said, as if he were looking at a rainbow.

Matt said dubiously, "Do you really think we can fix it, Dad?"

Becky said, "I want to see where I'll sleep."

Andy said hopefully, "Gee, there's going to be room for a basketball court!"

Mr. Judge stared at his new home and turned his back on it.

Liza stalked up the steps to the veranda feeling as if the sky had fallen. But when she got past the shabby siding and stepped inside the double door, blue and rose and golden lights glowed on the dusty floor. She gasped with pleasure and turned to see sunlight striking through stained-glass panels in the door. Unexpectedly, she was enchanted. The panels were designed with lilies and roses, and, she thought with a sense of fantasy that a house with stained-glass doors could not be all bad.

A stairway rose at one side of the hall, slim and elegant, with hand-turned rail and spindles, and a finely carved owl on the newel-post.

"Now I'll show you all how it's going to work," Dad was saying. "It's not too big for a family house. It has only eight bedrooms and two baths on the second floor. But the views are great. Now, down here we've got a nice living room—"

He opened a carved sliding door to show a square room with high ceilings, long windows with stained-glass panels at the top, and a hearth with a carved marble mantel. The woodwork was freshly painted, and the walls papered with a pale gray-blue paper.

"We just finished this room last week," Dad said. "Look how nice this woodwork is!" He ran his hand up the carved and fluted window trim lovingly.

"Eight bedrooms!" Liza was trying to digest the idea of such space. "What are we going to do with all those bedrooms?"

"Fix them up!" her father said cheerfully. "We can always find someone to live in them."

They went through another sliding door. "Neat!" said Andy, pushing the door in and pulling it out of the wall. Beyond was a room with a bay window looking out on the side yard. Liza looked at the rusting cars with disgust. Dad looked out over her head.

"Don't think about the cars. Someone can haul them away. Look out there"—he gestured in a wide sweep. "See the water? The sun sets out there."

When she looked afar, Liza saw the water vista with the sun dancing on the ripples, islands in the distance, a white ferryboat moving toward them, a tug hauling a log boom south from Canada.

"The view is much better from upstairs," Dad said. "This is a family room here, and here's a room and bath for Gram when she comes. And this room here"—he led them across a square empty space with a dark and dirty fireplace in one wall—"this will be the dining room. And this way to the kitchen."

The kitchen was another shock. Liza looked from an old wooden icebox to the porcelain sink worn through to rusting iron, to the linoleum, shredding around the edges and broken in the middle of the floor, to the stove . . .

"Dad, how does that stove work?" she asked suspiciously.

"It takes a little practice." He grinned at her. "Actually it's a good old iron wood stove, and it'll be very handy if the power goes off. But look at that nice old table which was in the house!"

The round oak table had a carved pedestal with claw feet. Liza had never paid much attention to furniture, but that old table was inviting. She liked it.

"And here's a back stairs." He opened a door at the back of the kitchen, and they all went up the stair that curved up to the next floor.

"Great!" pronounced Andy. "We never had a back stairs before."

Becky followed her family in silence, with Mr. Judge at her heels. Liza was curious about what she might find, and from the second-floor hall she opened a door to discover another stair that went up to the third floor. She heard Dad telling the others they could choose their own rooms, and closing the door behind her, Liza ran up the steps and came out about the middle of the attic. To one side were a couple of small bedrooms at the front of the house. But at the far end of a passage she opened a door to find herself in the back of the attic, where a fireplace chimney rose through the roof beside a low dormer window looking out to sea. A perfect private corner!

"I've found an all-alone place," she whispered to herself, and exhilaration raced through her. Closing the door behind her, she ran down again to the second floor, where she looked at the room next to the attic stairs. It was smaller than her room in Seattle, but it was at the back of the house where it overlooked the water, and she liked the feeling of cozy space and being close to the stairs and her all-alone place.

Dad's bedroom was a big room on the west side of the house, overlooking what Dad said would be a garden someday. The room had a fireplace, faced with blue-and-white Delft tiles, and a bay window over the "garden," and it was decorated and finished. "I've been living here since I bought the place," Dad said "about a month now. I figured I'd do this room first and work out from here. And now you're all here, we'll all work till the house is finished."

He had found a retired fireman named Rod, who

had a carpenter friend, and both had been working on the house the past month. Rod came over that first Saturday afternoon and told the Mackays, "We'll have you in and settled before the Fourth of July. How's that?"

"Great!" Don told him. "That's Matt's birthday. We'll have something extra to celebrate."

"I like to have a date to aim at," Rod said cheerfully. "Somehow you always come closer than if you don't."

In the next days he showed all of them about scraping, sanding, cleaning surfaces for paint; about sweeping up dust as they worked; about looking for spots that needed attention; painting evenly and neatly; and about being critical of their own work.

Liza worked hard, even though she disliked it. She found that if she kept busy enough, she could forget lonesome memories. It seemed to take forever to sand and scrape and try to please Rod. She felt strange in this town, and wondered if she would ever find a friend. Then one day Rod said, "That door is ready for paint. You did a real good job there."

Even if nothing else happened, she told herself, at least she had learned how to take paint off wood and get it ready for another coat. She hoped she would never have to do a job like that for the rest of her life.

But when the curtains were hung and her clothes put away in the freshly painted closet and there was nothing more to do, Liza looked around and that sense of being lost or misplaced hit her anew. She longed to talk to her best friend back home and tell her about the all-alone place. Fixing up that place would be comforting.

She worked on her space, in between helping Becky finish with her room and then Andy with his room, and, without anyone's noticing, she managed to dust the floor and walls, clean the dormer window, and fit an old bolster pillow in the chimney corner, her dollhouse beside the window, and her favorite stuffed owl near the bolster for company.

The last Sunday in June they were enjoying their first meal in the finished kitchen, resting up from the week's work. The new steel sink, electric stove, and refrigerator-freezer were all in place. The new tile on the floor was a handsome pattern in yellow and black. Liza was looking at the farm-life pattern on the wallpaper, not sure how she liked it, when Dad said casually, "I've asked a friend to come by this afternoon and get acquainted with my family. She is Maggie Duncan, and she has three kids about your ages. I think you'll like her.

"I went out to fix her refrigerator last April. She teaches sixth grade at the school Becky and Andy will be going to, and she said she'd like to know you." He looked self-conscious. "I said, 'Just let us get the house organized a little first.' So I thought this might be a good day for her to come and see you all."

Liza looked at Matt. Dad had found a "new friend" who had three children of her own and wanted to meet Dad's kids?

"Is she nice?" Becky was asking.

"You bet she's nice!" Dad sounded delighted.

Liza, startled, was sensing like photoflashes all the possibilities: dating—marrying—new mother. She had kids—stepmother, stepbrother, stepsister. Maggie Duncan . . . What do you call a stepmother?

Dad said, "I told her we'd celebrate getting the kitchen finished and go out for dinner." He smiled at Liza. "I think you deserve a break from this picnic cooking we've been living on, Liza."

She could feel building up once more all the fears and tensions of unexpected change. She had never thought of Dad's marrying again. Someone should have told her sooner, so she could have time to get ready. As soon as she could slip away, she went up to her all-alone place and huddled there, looking out beyond the trees to the water, trying to think through what would happen next . . . trying not to think. The water was deep blue under the sun, with tiny white ruffles scudding across the surface in a brisk wind. A white sailboat, about the size of the *Tinker Bell,* was heeling in the wind and racing across the water.

Within an hour Liza was going to meet Maggie Duncan, and she had no idea how she was going to feel. She knew how she should behave to a friend of Dad's. But that said nothing about how she was going to feel inside, deep down, when the moment came.

She went downstairs to her room and began changing her clothes reluctantly. She hated to dress up. Being fat was even worse in a dress than in jeans. She wondered if Maggie might be plump. Older women often were. It would be comforting to have another overweight in the house. She hoped with a desperate hope that Maggie was going to be fat. And jolly. Laugh a lot.

She heard noises of arrivals, greetings, laughter. It sounded like old friends back home. And, confident for a moment, Liza brushed her black hair, put on a blue headband that picked up the blue in her eyes, looked at herself in the mirror in her most becoming dress, and felt good about her looks for the first time since she had left Seattle.

She ran downstairs, and Dad said, "Maggie, this is my oldest daughter, Liza. She's been taking care of the family all these months. Liza, Maggie Duncan."

Liza looked at Maggie Duncan, and her heart sank hopelessly. Maggie was about Liza's own height, with windblown chestnut hair. She looked young and chic . . . and slim. Liza stuck out her hand, feeling clumsy and dowdy, and said, "How do you do, Mrs. Duncan?"

Maggie smiled with an expression that was both hopeful and uncertain. "I'm glad to know you, Liza. I hope you'll like living here." Liza could recognize in that smile that Maggie Duncan wanted Liza to like her and wasn't sure she would.

"It's going to be okay, I guess," Liza said, unsmiling. "Living here, I mean."

She wasn't sure at all that she was going to like Maggie. You can't like people just because your dad wants you to. Then she caught her father's eye, and he was looking unhappy with her. Probably she should be trying harder to act as if she loved every minute of this ordeal. But how could she act a lie? she asked herself resentfully.

"We came here from Tacoma three years ago," Maggie was saying as if she were trying to keep things going. "We just love it here." She turned to her family. "Here's Jennie," she said. "This is Liza, honey."

Liza tried to smile at Jennie, holding out her hand politely, and hating her at once. Jennie was just as thin and pretty as her mother, only more blond, and she had an expression that Liza immediately considered aloof, as if she knew she would be bored with these Mackay kids.

"And here's Steve," Maggie said.

Liza looked from Jennie to her brother and stared at the best-looking boy she had ever seen. He was tall and blond, with a stunning profile. She smiled at him eagerly and saw with painful recognition the same expression she saw on every boy she wanted to know. He smiled politely and said, "Hi, Liza. Nice to know you." But there was none of the gleam of response she hoped for, none of that glance that says, Gee, I'd like to know you. Nothing but a cool smile, showing white teeth. And after his greeting, Steve turned to Matt.

"Where'd you get that crazy pooch?"—gesturing to Mr. Judge.

Mr. Judge looked at Steve with his mournful expression, and Steve laughed at him. "What a character!" Then Mr. Judge waddled over to him and sank against his leg with a sigh.

Oh, well, what did I expect? Liza asked herself.

26

Maybe Mr. Judge will bring us together.

"Is everyone ready to go out for dinner?" Dad looked at the Mackays.

Liza was pessimistic now. It was going to be an ordeal, just as she had expected. But somehow the dinner got off to a better start than she had feared. Andy Mackay sat next to Tommy Duncan at the family table in the restaurant, and within ten minutes they were giggling and teasing each other and spilling food until the parents put Becky between them, and then the three giggled together. Jennie sat next to Matt and told him about the high school. Once she said, "It's nice here, really. People are friendly." And when she smiled, once, the smile was unexpectedly wistful.

Liza was trying to think of something that would get some response from Steve, and suddenly she thought of a question that seemed a blaze of inspiration. Show interest, get him to talk about himself! All the advice columns said the same thing.

She asked brightly, "How did you happen to come here from Tacoma?"

He seemed to freeze. And then he acted as if he hadn't heard the question and began to talk about the high school and all the things he did there. She watched him admiringly. He was looking across the room away from her. But with that profile and the lift of the head that reminded her of an eagle—she could have listened forever.

"What about dessert?" Dad was waiting to write the orders.

Maggie said, "The strawberry whip here is delicious. I'll have that—"

Liza said, "Dessert? I've been thinking about a cold fudge sundae all day."

There was a small silence, which probably meant nothing. But Liza was sensitized to silences about what she was eating. Why hadn't she asked for the strawberry whip? But she wasn't going to start eating to please Maggie Duncan, no matter what. Steve ordered a fudge sundae, too, and Liza felt as if that was a vote of confidence. Yet it didn't really taste all that good. And the strawberry whip looked like pink snow on a hot summer evening.

All the way home Liza felt the sinking despair that attacked her so often, wondering, Why can't I ever do anything right? and hating Maggie for being there—and trying not even to think about Steve, because her heart raced too fast when she did.

3

IN THE QUIET EVENING after the Duncans had gone,
Liza sat on the front steps of her home. The yard was
littered with crumpled papers, popsicle sticks, tabs
from soft-drink cans—even a couple of cans. There
was a newspaper blown against the fence. It had
been there since they had arrived. The ground was
hard and barren, as if someone had played basketball
on it for ten years. Liza thought again of the back
garden in Seattle, where heather foamed over the
rock garden, and the moonlight broom was a pale-
yellow shower of bloom. The hummingbirds were
darting around the honeysuckle that last week. Here
she had seen no hummingbirds.

She put the memory out of her mind and got up
to join her father, who was moving around the yard
with a big plastic bag, picking up scraps and litter.
Liza pulled the newspaper away from the sagging
wire fence and took it over to him to put in the bag.

"Mrs. Duncan seems nice, Dad."

"I'm glad you think so. How'd you like the Duncan kids?"

She shrugged and bent down to collect the cans.

"They're okay, I guess. That Jennie isn't my type at all."

"Liza, I told Matt this afternoon, and I'll tell you now: Maggie and I want to get married before the end of the summer. We both want you kids to get along, and we think you'll all be better off in one big family with two parents than the way things are now. Maggie will make a good home for us . . ."

Irrationally Liza felt that he was saying she had not made a good home for them. And, as if he read her thoughts, Dad said, "Liza, you've been doing such a great job of housekeeping and cooking I almost forget you're still only a young girl. You're entitled to have a family with two parents, and a mother who can help you with your problems."

She wanted to yell, I don't need anyone to tell me about my problems! And then she thought about Steve. He'd be part of her family, not any relation, really. He had hardly noticed her today, but, for goodness' sake, with all the rest of their lives together . . .

Dad said, "This means a great deal to me, Liza. I've been very lonely without Mom. I loved her very much, and maybe that's why I want another wife—because we had a good life together, and I can't go on alone."

"Well, I guess so," Liza mumbled. She was embarrassed by his emotion, but underneath she really did want Dad to be happy. "But I don't think I can call her Mom," she said. "I'm out of practice. And she won't really be my mom anyway."

"The Duncans feel the same way," Dad said.

30

"She wants my kids to call her Maggie, and her kids will call me Don."

"So when are you getting married?"

"We're thinking about the middle of August. A private ceremony in Maggie's garden, with just the two families and the two grandmothers. We've already alerted them, and they're both pleased."

"Okay."

There didn't seem to be anything more to say, not even to ask about. Her brain was numb with the new idea. It was going to take time to get used to it. And she just didn't know about Jennie.

"Liza?"

"Yes, Dad?"

"Look, honey, we know what it's like to bring two families together, and you kids may not like each other all that much for a while. All I want to say is, just try to be nice, will you, Liza? You can make people feel good when you want to. Just remember this: Maggie's kids have gone through trouble, too. If you'll just make up your mind to be nice to everyone, no matter how you feel, it will help us all."

"Dad, I won't be a hypocrite!" She was outraged, the more so because she hadn't figured out how she was going to act toward Jennie Duncan, let alone live with her in the same house.

"Liza, kindness is not hypocrisy! All I'm asking you to do is just to hide your unkind feelings and show a pleasant face."

"But that's so phony!"

He took her chin and turned her face to his. "It is not phony to be nice to people instead of hurting them. If you act friendly, you'll feel friendly. Of course it isn't easy. But you can make your feelings honest by caring as much about someone else's feelings as you do about your own. If you make the Duncans unhappy, you will be unhappy, I will be unhappy, and someday you will be more sorry than you can imagine."

"Oh, all *right!*" Liza cried impatiently. "Why do you always worry about how I'm going to act?" She twisted her chin out of his fingers and turned away, insulted.

"Because I've seen you in action a couple of times," her father told her. "In a new town and soon with a new family I want us all to start over again and have a good life."

Becky and Andy came running across the ragged turf with Mr. Judge, and her dad picked up Becky. "Maggie says she loves Mr. Judge, Becky. She's going to marry me, and she's so glad to be getting a good dog like that with me!"

Becky hugged her dad and hid her face in his neck. "Are we all going to live together pretty soon, Dad?"

"About six weeks," he told her, setting her down.

"That's good. I like Maggie."

Liza stalked away. Everybody liked Maggie. And it made Liza feel like a pig, when Dad warned her like that. She couldn't help it, could she, if she didn't like somebody like Jennie Duncan? She went inside the house and climbed up to her all-alone place, where she had added a few more things nobody wanted—a ragged upholstered footstool and a small battered table. There was a row of the books she loved when she was small, so she could go back to the time when everything was good and right and dependable—a nursery rhyme book with pictures, the Little House books, *Harriet, The Spy*. She settled into the chimney corner, reaching for Stuffed Owl, stared out of the window at rose and violet clouds, misty against a turquoise sky, and thought about Maggie. She would have to hide from Dad the way she felt about Maggie taking Mom's place. The trouble with Jennie was that Liza was going to feel inferior every time they were together. But on the other hand, there was Steve.

Just recalling his profile at the dinner table that night made her heart drop with a thud, and she held herself tightly, arms wrapped about the owl and around her shoulders. She had never felt like this about a boy before. Oh, there had been a fleeting crush on that black-eyed boy in fifth grade. And a kind of special interest in a redheaded boy who was in both seventh and eighth grades with her. She had dreamed about him sometimes, though he had never really paid any attention to her. But Steve . . . this feeling was real. It was physical—like her heart thumping whenever she thought about him. She wondered what it would be like to have him in the house all the time. Could she stand it? But she'd get used to it, she'd have to. Right this minute, she couldn't even care about his not noticing her. Just having him in sight was enough. Purely dazzled, she stared at the stars which were appearing, faint in the fading light, and found the first bright one—"Starlight, star bright, wish I may, wish I might have the wish I wish tonight." She wondered how soon she might see Steve again.

"I asked Maggie if she and her family could join us for a day on the *Tinker Bell*, for Matt's birthday party," Dad told his family at supper on Wednesday. "She said she'd like to bring the picnic food, and they'd love to be on the boat. They haven't been on one since they moved to Avalon."

Liza felt protest welling up and wanted to cry out, Why do we have to have them on Matt's birthday? But she saw the satisfaction in Dad's eyes, and Matt's anticipation of a real birthday party, and she set her teeth and thought about seeing Steve again.

"That sounds great, Dad," she managed to say. "We haven't been out in the boat . . ." she hesitated, thinking of Mom, and went on, "for an awful long time. Where will we go?"

"There's a nice little state park on one of the islands not too far from here," Dad said. "Okay, then. I'll tell Maggie to join us at the boat at ten o'clock, on the Fourth. She said she'd like to bring the birthday cake."

Liza sighed and looked at Matt, but he was staring out the window. Last year she had made the birthday cake. But last year had been a sad celebration. Okay. So she wouldn't make a cake this year.

The Fourth was a beautiful day, with clouds rolling gently across a brilliant sky, and the wind just ruffling the water enough for good sailing. The two families met at the marina at ten.

"Steve is sorry he can't come today," Maggie explained. "He's got this job, here at the marina, and this is one of their busiest days."

The day was going to be wasted, Liza thought. But, reminding herself that she was not going to make Dad feel bad, she climbed aboard like a heroic martyr, hiding her emotions gallantly. Dad was not even noticing. He was taking Maggie around the boat to show her where everything was and how it worked. Liza took the supplies into the galley and put them away.

Tinker Bell was a forty-foot ketch that Don had picked up twenty years ago at a great bargain. She was twenty years old when he bought her, he told Maggie with great pride, and he had repaired and improved and remodeled and mended ever since.

"She's a beautiful boat," Maggie said. "The boat we had was power, and I love sailing."

Andy and Tommy followed Matt around as he handled the lines and told them about sails and wind and navigation and tides. Maggie sat at the tiller, and Don showed her the compass and wind gauge and knot meter. Jennie lay down on a sunny spot of deck and closed her eyes. Liza sat in the cockpit with Becky, watching the quiet waters and the gulls soaring overhead and clouds scudding before the wind. It was good to be sailing again. It was almost like being alone.

They reached the island some two hours later and went ashore in the dinghy, in three trips from where *Tinker Bell* was moored to a buoy. It was a quiet little cove, full of rocks and driftwood and entirely alone. Liza climbed over a couple of driftwood logs and made her way up the steep bank, where she looked back down to the beach. Maggie was setting out boxes and packages and bowls of food on a picnic table. Matt was showing the younger boys what kind of wood to collect for a fire. Jennie looked up at Liza, but Liza turned and followed a path into the woods. She didn't feel like talking to Jennie.

She followed the path, which led through dense woods and up a rocky hill where she could look out across the water to forested mountain ranges against a sunlit sky. The solitude and the quiet sounds of the forest were like healing salve for her heart. She turned and walked slowly along the path, stopping to watch a goldfinch dart to a high branch, where it sat and poured out song. She touched the velvety emerald moss on a fallen tree as she listened and then moved on along the path. When she turned at a sharp angle, the scarlet twisted trunk of a madrona tree bent across the path just above her head. The sun caught the polished leaves and glinted into her eyes. She touched a trickle of pitch that had dried on the trunk of a Douglas fir, and pressed her fingers together and separated them, smelling the spring-fresh pine tar as she walked.

When she had circled the island and come back, Matt was talking to Jennie at the picnic table. He said he was going to be a sophomore in the fall, and Jennie said Steve would be a senior. Liza moved closer to hear about Steve. She put a hot dog on a stick and held it over the fire as she listened.

"He hates school," Jennie said. "Maybe because he's had bad luck with a couple of his teachers. But he really hates it."

"That's too bad," said Matt. "I thought he said he was into a lot of clubs and things."

"Oh, he is," Jennie said. "But he may have to drop his favorite one if he fails another course." She shook her head. "He's so crazy about boats—somehow that's all he's ever wanted to do. He hated to miss today, except that at the marina he's working with boats anyway, and sometimes he gets asked to be crew on some big boat."

Liza found a bun for her hot dog, spooned potato salad onto her plate, and sat down at the table. Andy and Tommy were toasting their third hot dog each, and Becky was helping Maggie pick up some of the scraps. Liza watched, feeling a little guilty about not helping, but she didn't feel like helping or talking much either. Jennie said to her, "Matt tells me you used to cook for your family in Seattle. Did you like it?"

Liza said indifferently, "It was okay," and filled her mouth with another bite of her hot dog so she wouldn't have to talk.

Matt said, "Come on, Jennie. Let's take a walk," and they left the table. Immediately Liza felt guilty, and then she was angry about feeling that way. And there was nothing she could do about it.

The boys took pails and shovels and set out to dig clams where the low tide uncovered sandy beds. In

37

a fit of conscience, Liza helped Maggie pack up for the return trip and took Becky to look for small pieces of driftwood to make a mobile. When they returned with a satisfactory collection of the twisted bits, the boys had filled buckets with clams, and Maggie, looking at them, said, "Beautiful, boys! Don, why don't you all come to our house tomorrow night for clam chowder?"

And Don said, "My favorite meal! Wonderful!" And then, "What happened to the birthday cake?"

"We've been separating and roaming around so, we haven't been together to have it yet," Maggie told him. "How about in the cabin on the homeward sail?"

And Liza, eating birthday cake with great relish, had to admit the day had been good, she was glad she was there. The cake was even better than the ones she made. And perhaps Steve would be home for the clam chowder supper tomorrow.

4

THE DUNCAN HOUSE was surrounded with flowers outside and it was pretty inside, with flowers on the tables, pale-green carpeting on the floor, sheer curtains at sparkling windows, a magnificent trailing fern hanging in the stairwell. Liza shrank a little inside at the contrast with her own home.

The next thing she noticed was that Steve was not there. Again.

Perhaps he didn't like the Mackays. But if his mother was going to marry Dad, how was having Steve in the family going to work?

"Would you like to look around the rest of the house?" Jennie asked her. "Tommy already has Andy up in his room."

"Sure."

Liza followed Jennie up the stairs and through the hall to see Maggie's bedroom and the boys' room, where Liza peered intently for any sign of Steve. "There are only three bedrooms, so Steve and Tommy have to share a room," Jennie said. And then they stopped in Jennie's room, and Jennie closed her door.

"I thought maybe we could talk better up here," she said. "Mom says she's going to marry your dad."

"I know," Liza said. "Dad told us last week."

Jennie shook her head. "I think your dad is just great," she said. "I'm awfully happy for Mom." She hesitated, as if some other question worried her. Then she said, "Oh, well, it's got to work out!" and turned to her bookshelves.

"You've got a lot of books," Liza said a little uneasily. She was not used to shelves of books except in the library.

"Oh, I love them!" Jennie was suddenly alight with interest. "Did you ever read this one?"

She held out *The Innocent Wayfaring*, and Liza leafed through it politely.

"It's one of my favorites," Jennie said. "About a girl in the time of Chaucer—way back, when pilgrims were going to Canterbury."

Liza had never heard of Chaucer or Canterbury. She closed the book and set it on the shelf, feeling out of her depth. "You like stories about olden times?"

"Oh, I love them best of all!" Jennie sat down and said thoughtfully. "When I really want to get away from all the hassle around here I like to get into a book about olden times. I can forget everything— for a little while." She looked wistful, as if she regretted having to come back from the olden days, and Liza listened, recognizing with surprise that Jennie had a private place of her own. They had something in common.

"You mean, you have a lot of hassle too?" she asked tentatively.

40

"Well—I worry about Steve a lot."

"I suppose he's working at the marina again to-night?"

"Probably. When he isn't at the marina, he's with Kim. Only, no matter what he's doing, he never seems to be happy, and he talks about getting out of the whole thing. He talks to me more than to Mom, or, anyway, I've heard him more than she has. I know she'd worry if she thought he might just take off any day . . ." She poured it out as if it was a relief to talk to someone.

Liza listened silently, not sure when to ask a question, wondering what was really behind Jennie's worry. And who was Kim?

"You said he didn't like school?" she ventured.

Jennie shook her head. "He hates school more than anything."

"How long has he been going with—Kim?"

"Oh, since about last Easter," Jennie said. "She's a senior this fall, too. She was in his English class, the one he had trouble with. She told me once, when she was over here, that she thought it really wasn't all Steve's fault, and she wished he wouldn't take it so hard. And then she helped him a lot—they studied together almost every night. But he still hates school, and it really worries Mom."

"Does Kim work at the marina, too?"

"She waits table in the restaurant there in the summer."

Jennie turned to her bookshelf and picked up *Jonathan Livingston Seagull.* "Did you ever read this one? It helps me a lot. It just makes me feel good,

41

as if I could do anything I had to, even—"

Somewhere a bell sounded, and Jennie jumped up.

Even what? Liza wondered.

"That's Mom's dinner bell. I guess she's ready for us."

Without Steve there were eight at the table. Maggie served the chowder from a big flowered tureen and passed pilot crackers with it. And when everyone praised the chowder as a very special meal, Tommy and Andy took great credit, giggling at each other through the meal.

And then they all talked about the coming wedding.

"On August eleven," Maggie said. "That would give us about two weeks after the honeymoon to get ready for school."

They moved into the garden after supper, to see how the arrangements would work and to talk about getting the Duncans moved into the big house and the families used to being together before school began.

After that everything seemed to happen very fast. The Mackay house was finished except for the boys' bathroom. "Oh, well, it works," Don said cheerfully. "We can always make a special project of it later." The garden was cleared of old cars and rubbish and planted with a few flowering rosebushes along a curving path laid out with rocky borders of heather and thyme. It looked sparse and bare compared to the Duncan garden, Liza fretted. But Dad said next year it would look very different.

The wedding day was racing toward them so fast that Liza felt they could never be ready. Gram Mackay arrived from Los Angeles and told her son this was the best news of the year. She took Liza and Becky out to find new dresses for the wedding, and Liza became melancholy all over again when she saw herself in so many mirrors.

Maggie's mother, Mrs. Baker, arrived, and both families had dinner and a festive get-acquainted evening together before the wedding to talk about final details. Steve was there that night, and he seemed cooperative about the plans and smiled once at his mother—as if something hurt, Liza thought, watching him.

Well, something was hurting her, too.

The wedding day was clear and sparkling and sunny. The mountains on the faraway horizon were clear shadows against a blue sky. The August air was fresh and sweet, with flowers crowding the garden and showers of roses against the house and fences.

The two families came together in the Duncan garden, smiling at each other. Liza had been nerving herself up all week to rejoice with her father—not let him know about her uncertainties, to be nice to everybody. She looked at Steve, standing with his chin up, his mouth tight, looking over the heads of his mother and Don. And she tried not to notice Jennie, who looked beautiful in a slim white dress.

The service was so short that Liza had hardly started listening when it was over. And then she found herself crying and not knowing why. Maybe because Dad looked so happy.

After the ceremony the bride and groom and the grandmothers toasted one another in champagne, and the bride cut the cake. Then Jennie took over the cake knife for her mother, and was filling plates when Liza came up to the table. She smiled at Liza warmly and said, "This is a very happy day for us, Liza."

Beside her, Steve held out a plate for cake and said, "Speak for yourself, Jennie!"

"I am!"

He moved away and Liza followed him with her plate of cake and ice cream. Now he was a stepbrother, part of her family. She felt as if she could talk to him now. She said, "My best friend's sister, back in Seattle—she was married last year, and she put a big chunk of wedding cake in the freezer to celebrate their tenth anniversary. Isn't that nice? Planning your tenth anniversary at the wedding? I wonder if Maggie would like us to put some of this away for her anniversary next year."

Steve looked at his cake gloomily. "I won't be around then. I wasn't all that keen on being here today."

"Are you going away?"

"I hope so!" he said, savagely hopeful. "I wrote my dad last week and told him I wanted to live with him, to finish school there. I might just cut out and travel down that way anyway. I don't know how long I can stand it around here."

Liza felt a kind of panicky turmoil inside when

she heard Steve say he was not going to stay around, as if she had been cheated. She had told herself so often that having Steve in the family was the thing that would make this marriage worthwhile. So if he was gone, how could she stand it?

It seemed very important to keep him talking.

"Where is your dad?" she asked.

For once, he didn't mind talking to her. "He's down in Brazil—a big executive down there. Soon's I hear from him I'll be on my way."

"Wasn't that a lovely wedding, Steve?" His grandmother Baker joined them, looking misty-eyed.

"Yeah. It was great."

He left them, and Liza saw him talking to Matt at the far side of the garden a moment later.

"And aren't you happy for your father?" Mrs. Baker persisted.

"Oh, yes," Liza tried to be enthusiastic. "I hope —well, you know—it's going to be a whole new life. For both of us. I mean for the Duncans and the Mackays."

"Oh, but it's going to be a happy one!" Mrs. Baker moved on to talk to the bride and groom again.

That's right! Liza thought savagely to herself. Keep the faith!

The festivities were ending. Dad and Maggie drove away in the Mackay car to spend ten days on the Olympic Peninsula, and Steve disappeared somewhere. The boys were clamoring for more cake and ice cream, and the grandmothers were again congratulating themselves that their families had found each other. And then everyone began to clear the garden. Each person carried something into the house—wedding cake, plates, glasses, chairs, tables, leftover food. And the Mackays prepared to go home.

Gram kept saying, "What a lovely wedding! I know you're all going to be very happy!" And Liza kept trying not to hear her.

At home, she sagged down on a chair in the living room in a party-is-over kind of depression, and Matt slumped on the couch, looking as if he had retreated into deep thoughts.

"I'd feel a lot better about the whole thing if it wasn't for Jennie," Liza said, grimacing.

"What's wrong with Jennie?" Matt sat up with a jerk. "She's a great kid! A really great girl!"

"Oh, I know!" Liza cried. "That's what everyone says! Dad says just think about other people's feelings, and you'll love everyone. I don't believe it!"

"I'd feel better myself if it wasn't for Steve," Matt said forebodingly. "I don't know if I can ever like that guy."

Liza gasped. Not like Steve! She started to cry out, But why, for Pete's sake? Why wouldn't you like the only really good kid in the lot?

And then she closed her mouth firmly. Whatever Matt's reasons were she didn't want to know.

But it was an opening wedge between them where there had never been one before. If that was going to be Matt's attitude, they were going to be on opposite sides about the new family. And Liza would be on Steve's side.

5

THERE WERE THREE GOOD THINGS that Liza could
be glad about when she woke up the morning after
the wedding. One was that she wouldn't have to see
Jennie for ten days. The second good thing was that,
for the first time since she had moved to Avalon, she
didn't have to clean, polish, paint, or even dust and
sweep. And the third good thing was Gram's saying
that she could have the whole day off, just to celebrate. It was the kind of freedom she had not known
for—she could not count how long.

She wheeled her bike out of the yard at nine
o'clock in the morning to ride around and look at the
town and explore some shops and see what she could
discover.

She wheeled into Main Street and rolled along,
humming to herself, thinking about Steve moving
into their house in a couple of weeks. On a day like
this she could be optimistic, even about Matt's attitude.

At the crosswalk by a corner drugstore, as she
waited for the light to change, a small black cat with
white feet ran across the street, a car screeched to a

stop and struck a wirehaired terrier chasing the cat. The blow tossed the dog onto the sidewalk beside Liza, where he lay, limp and unresponsive, and the driver of the car rushed over to see what had happened.

"I couldn't help it!" the driver gasped. "He ran right in front of me! Is he dead?"

Liza was feeling for a heartbeat, and she said, "No, he isn't dead!"

"Thank God!" said the woman. "I feel just terrible. As if I'd hit one of my own kids! He was so cute and bouncy—"

A boy, white and terrified, rode across the street on a bicycle with a paper carrier and flung himself off to kneel down on the sidewalk beside the dog.

"He got away from me!" he said to Liza, sounding choked. "I couldn't stop him. Is he dead?"

Liza looked up at him and shook her head. He leaned over the dog, petting it, stroking its head, talking to it encouragingly. "Come on, open your eyes, old man. You're going to be all right. Isn't he?" he demanded of Liza.

"I couldn't feel any broken bones. But maybe we ought to carry him home."

"Oh, great! His name's Cockeyed Sam. See that black spot around one eye? Come on, Sam boy."

Liza gently tied her headband around the dog's muzzle. "He might snap instinctively," she explained. Then she took off her jean jacket and used it like a stretcher to slip under Sam, who winced and cried. She lifted the dog so it could ride in the boy's paper carrier.

"You know just how to handle him," the boy said with a note of relief. "What's your name? I'm Barney Applegate."

"I'm Liza Mackay."

He was about her age, she guessed, about her height, a little plump, with straw-colored hair falling around his ears and freckles on a round face. Not a cool type at all. Especially when she thought of Steve. But a nice kid, even if he wasn't cool. The most important thing about him was Sam.

"How'd he get away from you?" she asked.

"I was teaching him to heel to the bike," Barney said. "He's been doing great, and it's going to be fun to run him with the bike. But he saw a cat and took off."

Sam twitched again, opened his eyes, and tried to wag his stubby tail. Barney lifted him out of the basket and onto the ground, where he struggled to his feet, whimpered a little, and began to walk gingerly.

"Okay!" Barney said with great relief. "He's going to be all right!"

He put a leash on Sam and gave the headband and jacket to Liza. "I'll put Sam in the backyard and buy us a sundae."

"Great!"

They rode to Barney's house and left Sam in the backyard, where he curled up in the sun, and then pedaled back to Applegate Drugs and Pharmacy.

"We've got the best ice cream in town," Barney said. "What kind of sundae do you like? I can fix it for you."

Liza stood at the counter and watched him as he scrubbed his hands, slipped on a white apron, and picked up the scoop.

"You work here a lot?" she asked.

"Sure. Afternoons in the summer and after school. And weekends. Lots of the kids come here for our ice cream. How about it?"

He was holding the scoop expectantly as she studied the list of twenty flavors, struggling with herself. She wanted to lose about thirty pounds as soon as possible. But she hadn't had any ice cream since that cold-fudge sundae with the Duncans. That was weeks ago! And Barney was so proud about his ice cream that she hated to disappoint him. And after all, what difference did one sundae make?

"Make it peppermint-candy ice cream with chocolate sauce," she said.

He built up a huge dish with three oversized scoops of ice cream and a lavish pouring of chocolate sauce. Liza trembled with eagerness and hated herself for her weakness. He set the dish on the counter with another for himself, and he and Liza took their ice cream to a small table by the window in the corner.

Liza looked around the store. It was full of interesting counters, and above the gift cards she read a sign, "We're a friendly place—but not to shoplifters." She grinned at that and asked Barney, "Where are you in school now?"

"Going into high school in September. How about you? When did you come to Avalon?"

"We moved here in June. And I'm going to be a freshman too."

She ate her sundae in blissful indulgence. It was the best ice cream and the very best chocolate syrup she had ever tasted. And she contemplated Barney as she ate. He was pudgy, hardly taller than she was, and not good-looking at all. But she had the feeling that anything she tried to tell him he would understand. And it would be kind of relaxing to have a boyfriend who didn't even notice how much she weighed, someone who gave her ice cream like this. She scooped the last drop of chocolate syrup out of her dish.

"I've got to get home now. Gram's going to think I fell off a cliff or something. That was definitely the best ice cream I ever ate, Barney. Thanks a lot."

"Where do you live?"

She described the old frame house.

"Oh, that must be the old Gibbons place."

He rode home with her, rode around the yard, and said, "Is this where you live? Honest? How come?"

"Well, we needed a lot of room." She wasn't ready to talk about the new family yet. "And Dad said we could fix up this place. You should have seen it when we got here!"

"I did! I wondered what kind of people were going to live here. But it looks great now. Really great. I never saw roses here before. You must of fixed it up a lot."

"We all worked all the time—like all summer,"

Liza said. And she realized, it really was fun to remember.

"The only thing that worries me now"—she was putting the worry about her stepfamily into the back of her mind—"is what the school will be like. Back home I had lots of friends. But here it's going to be different. How do I know if I'll find any friends?"

"I shouldn't think you'd have any trouble," Barney said. "I mean, all you had to do was help my dog when he got hit, and here we are, friends!"

"That's nice," she said again. "Well, thanks for the sundae, Barney. It really was the best I ever ate."

"I'll fix you another any time," he said, grinning at her. "I better go now. These advertising papers were supposed to be out before noon."

"Bye, now!" She watched him wheel down the sloping walk to the sidewalk.

"Be seeing you!" He disappeared around the corner.

Gram was setting out bread and butter and peanut butter and jelly for lunch for the younger Mackays when Liza came into the kitchen. She told Gram about Barney and Applegate's drugstore, and Gram smiled at her enthusiasm.

"I must say it's nice just to ride around and see the flowers," Liza said. "After all that painting and decorating, I don't care if I never paint another house."

"But the job you all did on this place is some kind of miracle," Gram was saying. "I thought maybe I'd put a few plants in the yard for a wedding present.

I found a good nursery this morning."

"What a nice idea!" Liza glanced out of the window. Even with the rusting old cars gone, the yard didn't look like much. But the roses were in full bloom, and the rock-bordered path looked as if it wanted to go somewhere. "What did you find?"

"I saw a couple of holly trees. And a Japanese maple. Are there any special plants you think Maggie might like?"

"I never heard her say."

"Well, there's plenty of time to choose things."

It did seem like plenty of time—ten days—before the Duncans would be moving in, before Dad and Maggie would be coming home. Gram took Liza out to the nursery to choose some of the plants, and for the first time in her life, Liza found herself becoming interested in arranging a garden. She found a pot of lavender, and the fragrance took her back to the Seattle garden. She wanted to plant at least two patches of lavender for old times' sake.

Gram bought two holly trees and half a dozen flowering bushes, including some rhododendron. Back at the house she and Liza did the planting. It took several days to finish the garden, but Matt helped with the digging, and Becky and Andy helped with the watering afterward. And then, all of a sudden it seemed, it was Sunday afternoon, and Dad and Maggie were coming home.

Helping Gram put lunch together for Matt and Becky and Andy, Liza tried not to think about the new life opening up within a few hours. But somehow she could not keep her mind from wandering into worry. She reminded herself that Steve would be moving into this very house. But now that made her uneasy rather than confident.

She went up to her all-alone place to look out at the afternoon sunlight smiling on the waters of Puget Sound and to arrange her thoughts and feelings to greet Dad. And her new stepmother. But nothing happened.

With a sigh she pulled herself together and went down to the kitchen for ginger cookies. They seemed to appease her nerves more than anything else at a time like this. Matt came in and got a can of Coke, and he must have been nervous too because he began nagging Liza about eating all those cookies. And that didn't help anything.

Then she heard the front door open. And Dad was home with his new wife. And Liza ran out to the front of the house, hugged Dad, looked at Maggie. And tried to act glad about her new mother.

6

IN THE NEXT COUPLE OF DAYS, Gram went back to Los Angeles and the Duncans moved into the Mackay house. Liza felt as if they were a visiting crowd of houseguests. Apparently the Duncans felt the same way. They were all carefully polite to each other, and everyone felt that living with so many strangers was a strain. Liza felt as if she were walking on ice that could send her skidding without notice.

Tuesday night, the first dinner after the Duncans had moved in, Maggie looked around the crowded table, smiling at the Duncans sitting on one side and the Mackays on the other, and said, "Let's take hands around the table, everyone, and give thanks for being together."

Don was smiling at Maggie as he reached his hands to Jennie on one side and to Liza on the other. Liza could see that Dad was a little self-conscious. But she reached for Andy beside her and looked at Steve across the table to see if he was part of this friendship ring. He was looking at his mother without smiling, as if he really didn't like it.

Maggie raised her hands, holding Steve's and

Matt's, and said, "From this day forward we're a family. One for all and all for one!" All of them around the table raised joined hands, looking at the other's family and smiling, and then they settled back, and Don began to serve the plates. Liza thought about the little ceremony, like a grace. She felt better about her new family in spite of herself.

Over blueberry tart dessert, Maggie looked at Don and said, "Perhaps this is a good time for all of us to talk about the things that have to be done around the place and who will do them."

He nodded. "You tell the girls your ideas, Maggie."

"I thought it might be easier if I do the cooking, Liza. You won't have to think about getting dinner for nine people when you get home from school. And you may have things you'll want to stay late for."

"Fine," Liza said automatically. She felt funny in a mixed-up way, as if she were being pushed out of her kitchen. And yet she knew well enough that if she had to cook dinners for this big family, she would have felt that that was unfair, too.

"Jennie, you and Liza can make your own arrangements about how you want to handle the cleanup at the end of the day, taking turns however you want."

Jennie grimaced, half teasing. "The more it changes, the more it's the same, isn't it, Mom?" She shrugged as if she was resigned to doing dishes for the rest of her life.

"And, Liza, you can arrange with Becky and Jennie about cleaning your bathroom. It should be clean and neat for the day when you go to school, and have a thorough cleaning once a week. Okay? The boys will take care of theirs the same way."

She smiled brightly, and Liza sensed that Maggie had been a little self-conscious about giving instructions to the Mackays. Maggie sighed as if a strain was past, and said, "Don, you've got a program going, too."

Don began explaining to the four boys about taking out trash and garbage every night, cleaning up the basement before school began in September, digging beds for planting around the house. "The place looks so good with the trees Gram planted while we were away, I want to get the rest of the garden started this fall. Next spring it can all be beautiful."

Steve was staring at Don with a dark hostility, and then he tightened his mouth as if it took all his self-control to keep from protesting. He glanced from Don to Matt to Liza with a measuring stare, and Liza knew as clearly as if he had announced it aloud that he didn't like Don Mackay and he didn't like this new family.

He said indifferently, "I have to be at work at the yacht club marina every day and weekends, you know."

"After supper, too?" Don queried. "That's the only time Matt and I are going to have for house and yard work."

"Okay." Steve sounded as if he didn't care what happened, and Liza looked down at her plate thinking. For the first time she wondered what had happened to Steve's father. It must have been a divorce. But did Steve ever hear from him? She was trying to figure out how she could ask without prying when she looked at Jennie and found her gazing back with a pleading expression. As if she hoped for understanding. As if she worried about Steve.

After supper, while they were organizing the work in the kitchen, Liza asked Jennie about their early years in Avalon.

"Mom was working awfully hard at first, getting qualified for teaching, and everything, and I used to get home earlier than she did, and then I'd get the supper for everyone. Most of the school days."

"Didn't she teach before?"

Jennie shook her head. "Not before we came to Avalon."

She said no more and Liza remembered Dad's saying last month, *"The Duncans have come through trouble too."* Now she wondered what kind of trouble it was.

In spite of herself, Liza felt irritable and defensive when Maggie took over. She would look at Maggie sitting at one end of the dining table, smiling at Dad, and feel that a stranger was invading the family. She liked Maggie, she kept telling herself. She liked Maggie, who was really nice. But still . . . She tried not to let her feelings show, not to sound irritable, not to let anyone know—especially herself. But now and then, late at night, she hated having another family and another mother in the house. And then she tried to put that feeling out of her mind, remembering Dad's warning about making people unhappy, and

58

being more unhappy herself if she did.

Jennie had a summer job, looking after a couple of small children, so she was gone most of the days. Liza didn't like Jennie, but she missed her in those long days when Jennie was busy and Liza was not. Liza spent a lot of time riding around the town, getting acquainted with shops, and often stopping at Applegate Pharmacy, where an ice-cream sundae always made her feel better.

The days ran swiftly into Labor Day weekend, and, on Friday of the holiday weekend, when she came in from riding around, Liza found Maggie sitting at the round table in the kitchen with a pot of tea and a cookbook.

"Oh, Liza, you're just in time! Pour yourself a cup of tea and help me decide what we want to take for a picnic somewhere with *Tinker Bell* for the last summer weekend."

"Okay." Liza poured herself a cup of tea. It did feel good to have someone drinking tea when she came in like this. She set the cookie jar on the table and sat down. Maggie glanced at the cookies as if she wanted to say something, and then went on with her menu planning.

"I'm thinking of potato salad and hamburgers and hot dogs," she said.

"Everybody likes those things," Liza said.

"But I'd like something different and special."

"How about blueberry pie for dessert?" Liza suggested.

"Good." Maggie wrote it down.

Steve came in the back door at that minute and opened the refrigerator as if he felt at home. "Hi, Mom, what's to eat?"

"Try peanut butter. We've got lots."

He poured himself a glass of milk, made a peanut butter and jelly sandwich, and sat down at the table, acting as if Liza were invisible.

"How was the marina today?" Maggie asked.

He took a long drink of milk, tipping his head back so the glass screened his face. "Okay. Why?"

"I thought you might have a lot of extra business this last week of summer."

"We did. Everybody within fifty miles took his boat out because it's such a good day. I was running all day long."

"Are you working tomorrow?"

"Tomorrow is likely to be worse than today. Why?"

"Don wants to go sailing all day, with a picnic at one of the islands."

"Sailing!" Steve set his glass down and folded his hands behind his head. "That *Tinker Bell* is a good boat!

"I'll tell them I've got to go to a funeral . . . or something," he said. "I'd like to handle *Tinker Bell.*"

Maggie looked uneasy. "Steve, you've got to be responsible about your job. If they're counting on you—"

"They can count on someone else for once," he said. "I haven't had a day off all summer." He drained his glass and got up. "I'm meeting the guys tonight," he told his mother. "See you later."

"But, Steve! Don asked you this morning if you'd get that yard cleared tonight with Matt, and you told him you'd be here. He wants it finished tonight so we can sail tomorrow and know it's done before school begins!"

"Okay, okay!" he yelled. "Don't keep bugging me about the damned yard!"

Liza winced. Steve, she wailed inside, don't be like that! Be nice to your mother!

Maggie ignored his tone and said firmly, "You can't just forget a job you promised to do because something else came up unexpectedly."

"Okay, *okay!*" he said again. "I'll be here for supper." He came around the table and gave his mother a hug. "You know I wouldn't let you down, Ma!" He grinned at her, and she patted his hand.

"Just don't disappoint Don, Steve. He's got a schedule for things to be done before school starts, and he's counting on you."

He nodded and went off, slamming the door behind him, and Liza drew a breath of relief. He really was nice to his mother, mostly. And everyone gets mad at parents some of the time. Only it was disillusioning to hear him yell at Maggie like that.

"Steve has had a rough time getting used to a new life," Maggie said, glancing at Liza. "It's been a hard adjustment for him."

Liza would have liked to hear more, but she wasn't sure what to say, and Maggie went back to her cookbook.

"Want me to make dessert for tonight?" Liza asked.

"What do you have in mind?"

Liza had in mind something that would strike Steve with such a wave of awareness that he would look at her with new recognition.

"Matt loves my chocolate pudding cake," she said.

"H'm," Maggie had her eyes on her cookbook. "Let me think about it. We're having macaroni and cheese tonight. How about floating island? Or mixed fruit?"

Liza shook her head. She knew how Steve felt about chocolate, and she had to make a chocolate dessert. "Dad never liked floating island much," she told Maggie.

"You make what you like."

So Liza made her chocolate pudding cake and served it proudly, with ice cream heaped on top.

Dad said, "Great dessert, Liza!" and ate two helpings.

Matt said, "Even better than usual!"

And Steve said, "Did you make this?" as if he could not believe it.

Maggie said, "Just a teaspoon of pudding for me, Liza." And when Liza gave her as much as she herself was eating, Maggie ate very slowly, saying, "This *is* delicious, Liza." And left three fourths of her serving.

But if she liked it, why did she leave so much? Liza knew why and tried not to notice it. Maggie had a pretty figure, and once she had remarked, "It isn't easy! I watch my weight all the time."

Sitting with her ice cream melting over her

chocolate pudding cake while she recalled that line, Liza was depressed again. One more dessert couldn't do that much damage. She ate a couple of mouthfuls. She would begin dieting tomorrow. Maybe with Steve in the house and Maggie watching her own weight all the time, Liza's pounds would fade away. Or maybe no one would notice.

In the end she laid down her spoon, leaving half the dessert on her plate and feeling both persecuted and heroic. Jennie cleared the table while Liza scraped dishes in the kitchen. Every time Jennie returned to the dining room, Liza ate another teaspoon of her leftover dessert. It was too bad to waste it. And yet she didn't really enjoy it as much as she used to. She ate one more spoonful slowly, and then, on an impulse, dumped the last third into the garbage. She finished up the dishes with a sense of having won some kind of victory.

Twilight was settling over the yard when Liza and Jennie went out to see how the boys were getting along. On the alley side of the tottering fence at the back of the lot, a stack of old scrap lumber, cartons, wire, and rusting tin cans reached the top of the fence. Matt came up from the basement, toting an immense carton—full of old rags, tangles of wire, and moldy bits of lumber. He dumped it outside the fence and went back to the basement.

"Last load!" he said, as he disappeared down the steps.

Andy was collecting rocks in a corner, and Tommy, looking for last scraps around the fence, came back puffing, with an armload of old branches.

Steve ruffled his hair. "You've been doing a good job of work, kids. Don't know how we could have done it without you."

Tommy looked up, grinning. "Remember when we had that yardman in Tacoma? He was always trying to get you to do some of his work."

Steve said, "Remember, pal! That's what we don't talk about."

"Oh, I know," Tommy said. "But why not?"

"Just follow orders and don't ask questions!" Steve snapped at him. Then he grinned. "That way you'll be ready for the Army when you join up!"

"Okay, chief!" Tommy saluted him and went off to fill his basket with another pile of litter.

Liza watched him go with a mixture of sensations. She liked the way Steve treated his little brother. She wondered why Tommy was not supposed to talk about the yardman in Tacoma.

The light was dimming, and Matt said, "Okay, troops. Put the tools away. It's been a good night's work, and Dad says we'll go sailing tomorrow."

"You've done a wonderful job," Liza said, hoping Steve would appreciate being appreciated.

"It wasn't all that much." Steve turned away as if he would rather not be noticed. And then he pulled his bike out of the rack and rode off to meet the guys.

7

THE FIRST DAY OF SCHOOL was golden with sun and fresh with the wind off the water. The whole family came together for breakfast, all of them excited about the opening of the school year.

Maggie told Andy and Becky about their new school.

"They have Cub Scouts and Brownies," she said. "They'll all begin by the end of the week."

Becky sat back, glowing with satisfaction, and Tommy said he'd show Becky and Andy the way to school. It was only six blocks from the house.

Steve talked about the high school as if he ran the place, and Matt ate his oatmeal as if he wasn't listening. But when Steve said, "Well, might as well be on our way," Matt joined him to ride bicycles together to the high school. A few minutes later Liza and Jennie rode off together.

They were within a block of the school when a couple of girls rode up alongside Jennie.

"Hi, Jennie! Did you have a good summer?"

"It was okay. My mom got married again. This is my stepsister, Liza Mackay."

"Hi!" Both girls smiled at Liza as if they were happy to know her, and they all walked into school together. The school seemed to be about the same size as her junior high in Seattle, Liza thought. Not too big. That made it more familiar. Jennie and her friends turned off at the first intersection to their freshman homeroom, and Liza went on alone to hers. The girl next to her was Marky Downs, and she was very friendly.

The teacher, Miss Wilson, smiled at the twenty-five freshmen before her, said they were all going to have a good year together, told them to come to her with any problems, and handed out programs with lists of books and supplies.

Liza went to math first period, social studies with Miss Wilson; study hall, where she saw Barney; and then to cafeteria, where she met Marky again. Over lunch they talked about teachers.

"Oh, you've got Miss Long for English!" Marky said. "She's terribly hard! My brother had her last year." She sounded very dubious.

Liza was dubious herself after that first class in English, which was her last class in the afternoon. Miss Long said, "We'll do a lot of writing in this class, and the assignment for tomorrow will be to write one good paragraph on what you hope to get out of your freshman year. Choose one subject and develop it in a paragraph of not more than a hundred words. Something you want to say to someone."

Liza recoiled at first. But by the end of the class she was beginning to think the assignment might be interesting. What she wanted most out of her freshman year was new friends.

At the end of the afternoon she read announcements on the bulletin board with Marky. Football players would meet at three fifty on the field. Liza wondered if Matt had seen that notice. Anyone interested in working on the school paper should come to the journalism office during the noon hour tomorrow. Tryouts for the fall play would be a week from Friday after school. The fall play would be *Our Town.*

They moved on toward their lockers, and, approaching the intersection, Liza saw Steve striding across the hall with a girl who was dark and thin-faced, and sparkling as she looked up at him. Liza wished she could get used to seeing him, so she wouldn't have that clutching sensation inside every time. And who was that girl?

Marky jabbed her with her elbow. "Isn't he the most gorgeous boy you ever saw? I saw him in the cafeteria this noon and I nearly swooned. My girl friend says she met him once last year, and he was really nice. She said he's not snobby or anything."

"Yeah, he's nice, I guess."

"You know him?"

"Kind of. He's my stepbrother."

"Wow!"

Barney came up and fell in step with them. "Hi, Marky. You going home, Liza? I'll ride along with you."

They talked about classes and teachers at first, and then Barney said, "Say, did I tell you what Jennie said to me this noon?"

Liza had a sinking moment. "I didn't know you knew Jennie."

"She's in my homeroom."

Liza determined not to care what Barney thought of Jennie. "So what did she say?"

"Her locker is near mine, and she was there when I was leaving my books for lunch. So I said I knew you, and she said she loves having a family again."

"Oh." Liza felt a lift again. "Well, that's nice. I —we like the Duncans just fine."

"She's a nice kid."

"Do you like her?" Liza could not help her voice sounding sharp.

Barney shook his head. "Oh, she's okay. Like I said, a nice kid. But she's not my type."

He might be sounding wistful, but Liza looked at him, and her smile broke out like the sun from behind a cloud. Jennie was not his type, he had said.

"So long. Thanks for riding over with me."

"Be seeing you!" He rode off.

Supper that night was full of news about the first day of school. Becky loved her new teacher and was excited about joining the Brownies. Andy and Tommy reported that their fifth-grade teacher had a funny name, and they were convulsed with giggles about it. But they liked him.

Liza said, "Miss Long said in English class that we have to write a paragraph for tomorrow—the very first thing!"

Tommy looked up brightly. "Oh, you got Miss Long? Steve had her last year." He leered at his brother impishly, and Steve scowled at him and said, "Shut up, Tommy!"

"What's she like?" Liza asked. "Is she really hard?"

Steve acted as if he had not heard her, and Tommy volunteered, "She flunked Steve last year!"

Jennie reached out to silence him, but it was too late. Steve glared at his little brother and said through his teeth, "She hated me, and nothing I could do was going to please her."

"But you said you wouldn't stay after school for that old cow!" Tommy remembered.

"Tommy!" Maggie said in a sharp tone Liza had not heard her use before. "That's enough! You have no business bringing up old troubles. Steve will be working as hard as anyone this year."

"Yeah, I bet!" said Tommy.

Liza knew how she'd feel if Becky said something like that about her in front of Steve. She'd die. Steve was pained and silent for the rest of the meal, and Liza suffered for him.

Over the dishes later she asked Jennie, "How did Steve like high school otherwise? I can see how Miss Long might be kind of rough."

Jennie shook her head. "He hates school, but I think it was Miss Long that put him off so much. He said he'd run away before he'd go to summer school. And he said he didn't even care if he didn't graduate—"

"But is he really not going to graduate next June?"

Jennie shrugged her shoulders. "I don't know—

yet. Kim Brown is very worried about it. She told me last summer that she was trying to persuade Steve to do the extra work, but he wouldn't touch it. And he's really crazy about Kim, but still she can't persuade him."

Liza's heart dropped so fast she felt faint.

"How did you get to know Kim so well?" she managed to ask. "You were only in eighth grade."

Jennie smiled knowingly. "But I'm Steve's sister, and she'd ask me things. And then sometimes she'd tell me little things that might help at home. She's really in love with him, and she's trying to make him see how important it is to graduate."

Liza thought drearily, What's the use of anything at all?

Aloud, she said, "Maybe this year will turn out better and he'll decide to catch up."

"Oh, he says this year is going to be okay except for studying. He's been asked to join the Mariners—all the cool guys are in that club, and he got to know them at the yacht club this summer."

"I wouldn't think Steve would have any trouble getting into any club he wanted to," Liza said, sounding more wistful than she knew. "He's so cool himself."

"I guess so," Jennie agreed. "The thing is, he took it real hard when Dad went off the way he did, especially after—Oh, well, Mom said not to talk about it because it just keeps hard feelings alive."

Liza was about to say, Oh, what happened? when she caught herself in time. But she spent quite a lot of time in the next days and weeks wondering what had happened to Steve's dad—wondering if Steve ever got the letter he was looking for.

And she spent a lot of time thinking about his not graduating. She had never known anyone who didn't want to graduate. It never occurred to her that there could be a choice. So, what happened to a dropout?

It made her very uneasy about Steve. He was so wonderful. And yet he kept surprising her with these strange and stubborn choices.

8

AFTER THAT FIRST WEEK, the school year seemed to move along very fast. Matt made the football team and his family attended every home game. Liza found herself greeting lots of people in the halls and in the cafeteria. And she got used to seeing Steve and Kim at the end of the day, walking toward their lockers, always deep in conversation, not looking for anyone to speak to.

She asked Jennie once, "What's Kim really like? She looks as if she'd be nice."

"She is nice," Jennie said. "I've always liked Kim. She talks to me sometimes, and I can ask her about some of my problems, and she understands. I told Mom I'd like to have Steve bring her over for dinner on my birthday, and she said that would be okay."

"When is your birthday?" Liza asked.

"Next Friday," Jennie said. "I'm going to be fourteen."

Liza began thinking about a birthday present. What Jennie really wanted was a cat, but Maggie had said they did not need a cat.

Thursday night, when the shops were open late, Liza went to the Silver Nutmeg to look for a present. A lady was arranging tiny glass animals on a glass shelf in the window, and Liza stopped to watch. The shopkeeper was pretty, with blond hair, long dark eyelashes, and a quick smile with dimples. Liza leaned her bike against a meter and went inside.

"Can I help you?" the woman asked.

"I'm looking for a birthday present for my stepsister." Liza felt self-conscious about not knowing what she wanted.

"Anything special?"

Liza shook her head. "I'd just like to look around."

She made her way around the shop, looking at ceramic flowers, picking up shell beads, looking at earrings and charms, and finding it hard to decide about anything. Maybe a charm? She turned the case with the silver charms slowly around, studying each one. There was a little silver cat, and she looked at it attentively, trying to detach it from the case. And then she was aware that the blond woman was watching her closely. It made Liza uneasy. She felt as if she ought to be saying something appreciative, or at least offering right away to buy something. Uncertainly, she turned the charm case again.

Two other customers came in, and the woman went to the other end of the shop to take care of them, and Liza let out her breath and relaxed. Now she could look around without having to decide too fast.

She looked at the dollhouse furniture on a round

table and picked up a tiny grand piano. It was a music box. Almost without thinking, Liza wound it up and listened to "Twinkle, Twinkle, Little Star," enchanted. It was fifteen dollars, and regretfully she knew she could not buy it. But she held it to her ear as she looked at the other miniatures: a marble-topped dresser with mirror, a nursery setting with a baby asleep in a crib, a Siamese cat curled beside the crib.

She thought of Jennie's feeling about cats, and picked up the china cat, wondering what Jennie could do with it. She felt something rub against her leg, and looking down she saw a live Siamese cat. In the shock of surprise she dropped the china cat on the carpeted floor.

Horrified she stood there, looking at the cat rubbing against her, and then stooped to pick up the china miniature. As she stood up she saw the shopkeeper moving toward her, looking stony tense. The china cat was unbroken, and Liza let her breath out slowly and set the cat down again beside the baby's crib with great care.

"I'd really like to have some of that doll furniture," she said, as if she were apologizing, and she edged toward the door.

The woman said, "Do you want that little piano?"

Liza looked at her hands and, astonished, found that she was still carrying the music-box piano. Embarrassed and flushed, she went back to the table and set it down.

"No, thanks," she said. "Not this time."

She could feel the eyes on the back of her neck as she left the shop, hot with embarrassment. And it was half a block later that she began to wonder if maybe that woman back there thought she was trying to steal something. Her throat caught, and she turned her bike and went toward Applegate's pharmacy. She had to talk to Barney.

She rushed inside and found Barney at the ice-cream counter, cleaning up, and the store almost empty.

"Barney! The most awful thing happened! I've got to talk to you!"

"What's the big crisis?"

"Well—" She looked around. "Have you got time right now? Look, I'll buy an ice-cream cone and sit here—till someone comes along."

He handed her the ice-cream cone. "What awful thing happened?"

"Well, I was shopping for a present for Jennie. Tomorrow is her birthday, and I've still got to find one. But I was in the Silver Nutmeg—" She told him of her shock about the woman's suspicions.

He nodded. "That's Miss Kapek. She's so suspicious about shoplifting that you can hardly walk past her window without her thinking you might pull something out by ESP. There was that thing last spring, when one of the kids did pull a shoplift in her store. He said he was getting a birthday present for his mom and was waiting to pay for it. But she said he carried it out of the store without paying and she called the police. It was a bad scene, and knowing him, I think maybe it was just the way she said. So she doesn't much like kids in her store."

"Who did it?" Liza was curious about details and wondered if she might know the boy.

Barney shook his head. "We don't talk about it around here. We figure the fewer people know about it the better. His mom was so upset—she told my dad about it—"

"But why would the kid do a thing like that?"

"Oh, some of the kids in the high school were into shoplifting last year, like a game, or something. They said they didn't do it for money, just for kicks. I know we lost some stuff—cameras and film. Things like that."

"But I still don't see why she had to think something like that about me!" Liza was outraged. "She never saw me before. She had no business being suspicious like that!"

"Well, some people in business get suspicious about any kid these days. Especially strange ones. How would she know?"

"Okay, I just won't go in there again," Liza announced, hoping that someday Miss Kapek would miss her patronage and beg her to buy something. That vision cheered her up so that she grinned at Barney. "So what can I do about a present for Jennie? I was just ready to get a charm for her bracelet, when Miss Kapek yelled at me about the music-box piano—"

"We've got charms," Barney said, going over to the counter next to the perfumes. "Same kind she has." He swiveled a case on the counter with bracelets in one panel and charms in two other panels. "Anything like this?"

"Yes!" she said. "That one right there! That's just what I wanted in the first place—a Siamese cat!"

He took the charm out of the case, found a tiny white box, and slipped it into a paper sack, and she paid him for it.

"Thanks again, Barney. You always make me feel better when I'm down."

She rode away, thinking about what a comfort it was to have a good friend like Barney, and she did not even think about Steve for the rest of the evening.

When she got home she wrapped the tiny charm, admiring the workmanship and wondering about starting a charm bracelet for herself.

So by Friday evening she looked forward to the birthday party with real enthusiasm. They had a festive ceremony before dinner, drinking ginger-ale punch while Jennie opened her presents. When she saw Liza's gift she cried, "Liza! Exactly what I wanted! How wonderful!" And Kim examined it appreciatively and said, "I love it!"

Kim seemed entirely at home with the Duncans and the Mackays. She asked Tommy how he liked fifth grade. She listened to Becky talking about the Brownies. She smiled at Liza and said, "Hi, there! How are things going for you now?" And she gave Jennie a neck ring with a polished rose quartz birthstone. Liza found herself liking Kim in spite of herself.

Jennie's birthday cake was especially rich and luscious, double chocolate with butter frosting, and

Liza, watching the lighted candles and Jennie making a wish, wished with her that she herself would be thinner before her own birthday. When Jennie blew out all the candles in a single puff, Liza felt that her own wish would come true as much as Jennie's would. And, on a wave of confidence, she left half her cake on the plate without even a struggle.

When dessert was finished and dinner over, Steve said, "We're going to see that movie at the Palace," and departed with Kim. And only then did Liza remember about Jennie's father in Brazil. Wouldn't you think he might have sent her at least a card?

9

ON SUNDAY AFTERNOON Barney rode up on his bike and asked Liza if she wanted to ride around for a while because it was such a nice day. They pedaled off together, admiring the madronas heavy with red berries and the huge golden leaves of the big-leaf maples.

"Where's Jennie today?" Barney wanted to know.

"She was going to give Becky a tennis lesson," Liza said. "Why?"

"Oh, I just wondered."

He turned a corner and Liza followed, talking about Jennie's birthday party. Barney seemed to be listening, but he said nothing. Then he turned another corner and said, "Let's watch the action on the tennis courts."

The only thing going on there was Jennie playing with Becky, and Barney wheeled alongside that court and sat and watched until play stopped for a moment. Then he waved.

Jennie came over to the fence. "Hi, kids! Did you see Becky's return there?"

"Very good," Barney approved. "Do you give lessons to just anyone?"

He grinned at her, and Liza felt as if she had stepped into a shadow. Jennie was not his type he had said only a few weeks ago. And now . . .

"I could use some of your coaching," he said.

Jennie smiled at him. "Why not? You want to play with us now?"

"I'll get my racket!"

"Nice kid," he said as they rode home.

And then he rode off, and Liza went into the house, feeling very sulky and not at all sure what to do about it.

When she came into the kitchen, Maggie was sitting at the table with papers strewn around and three cookbooks open.

"Hi, Liza," she said. "Everybody's busy this afternoon, so I'm working out menus while I have time."

"Okay." Liza sat down, still sullen but trying not to let it show.

"Look, honey." Maggie laid down her pencil and leaned her elbows on the table. "This is a good time for us to have a talk."

"Sure," Liza agreed. "What about?"

"Well, about menus. And calories. Honey, I know you'd like to be thin and wear size-ten dresses. I saw some of your pictures of a couple of years ago, and you had a lovely little figure."

"I know!" Liza moaned. "I guess it's just growing up. There's nothing anyone can do about it."

She sagged back with a deep sigh and looked out of the window. She hated to have anyone talk to her about her weight. She hated to think about it. All she knew was that it was a disaster she would probably carry around for the rest of her life, and the one thing she could not stand was talking about it.

"Now look, Liza"—Maggie was very serious—"you are only a young girl, you do not know all the answers. There are lots of things we can do. I've been thinking about the dinners we have. Starches and gravies and chocolate pudding three times last week. And sweet rolls for breakfast every day."

Liza jumped to her feet. "I won't listen!" she shouted. "You can't make me eat different things from everybody else! I won't do it! Nothing's been the same since you came into this family, and now you want to change me too—"

"But, Liza!" Maggie was aghast. "I'm only trying to help you, honey. You need someone to tell you some of these things."

But Liza had burst out of the room and was running up the back stairs, choking with fury and feeling the tears running down her face. She didn't hear Matt come into the kitchen and ask Maggie what had happened. She only knew she needed her all-alone place, and when she reached it she fell upon her pillow in the chimney corner, sobbing out her anger and hatred for herself.

When the sobs subsided, she sat up, mopped her eyes, and looked out into the darkening sky, her mouth set in stubborn determination not ever again to let anyone talk to her about her weight. She heard footsteps coming up the stairs and she stiffened again. Nobody was going to tell her what to do.

Matt opened the door and came over to her corner. He sat down on the floor, his arms around his knees.

Liza looked out of the window in a choking mixture of unhappy feelings—resistance, regret, sadness, anger, despair—wondering what Matt wanted, and not wanting to hear.

"Liza, what's eating you?" he asked. He sounded more angry than sympathetic, and she stiffened again.

"What business is it of yours?" She kept looking out of the window. "I don't want to talk about it."

"What were you yelling at Maggie about?" he asked. "I came in and there she was, feeling bad. She wouldn't talk about it either."

"What made you think it was me?" Liza asked angrily. "Am I the only one who makes everyone feel bad?" She turned and glared at Matt. "Did Maggie say it was me?"

"I heard you!" He glared back. "So what were you yelling at Maggie for?"

Liza lifted her chin and stared out at the lights in the distance.

"So what if I don't want to talk about it—What are you here for? I still don't want to talk about it."

"I don't know why you have to be like this." Matt was exasperated. "Sometimes you're just great. And then you get mad about something and kick people in the teeth."

"Did Maggie say that?"

"She didn't say anything about you. Only I could tell you hurt her feelings, yelling so I could hear it clear down in the basement. So why?"

"Well, I've got feelings too."

He looked at her with great scorn.

"What makes you think you're the only one in this family with feelings?" he demanded. "Time you thought about somebody else for a change."

"I've been nice to Maggie all along," she said. Her voice began to quaver again. "It wasn't really Maggie—" Tears began flowing.

Matt shook his head. "I sure don't understand you."

"Maggie said I was so fat she wanted to plan special meals for me!" Liza flung herself down on her pillow again and sobbed.

"But, Liza!" Matt protested. "Look, kid. Face it! You feel so bad about being fat you can't even talk about it. For Pete's sake, if Maggie can help you get over it, let her! Why yell at her?"

"Leave me alone!" Liza told him. But she wasn't yelling anymore, she was just sobbing. "Just get out of here, will you?"

"Okay, okay." Matt got to his feet. Then he said, "Maybe I shouldn't mention this, either, seeing how touchy you are about it. But I thought you were looking thinner the last couple of weeks. Like—your clothes look looser."

He went away and Liza lay where she was, trying to believe what he said. Matt thought she was thinner? She hadn't weighed herself since she had come to Avalon. She didn't dare to weigh herself now. But maybe . . . if Matt was right?

She composed herself, went down to the bathroom, bathed her face, and held a cold cloth against her eyes. She could hear the family gathering for dinner, and she began planning how she could face Maggie. Suppose she acted as if nothing had happened at all? She could not bring herself to planning meals, but suddenly she was not very hungry.

She went down to the kitchen, smiled brightly even though she felt self-conscious, and said, "Smells wonderful, Maggie." Suddenly she knew how to say it. "I didn't really mean to get so upset, Maggie. Just my mean old temper, I guess."

And Maggie said, "We'll both forget the whole thing, Liza."

And smiled at her.

10

THE BIG EVENT of the fall was the Halloween party on the school playground. There would be costume parades and prizes, ghosts walking, marshmallow roasts, games and fortunetelling—around several different campfires. Halloween fell on a Monday this year.

"It's really fun!" Marky told Liza, her eyes sparkling in anticipation. "I've got a new costume this year. And everybody wears masks. That makes it all the more exciting and kind of spooky. Be sure to look for me. I like the campfire closest to the woods."

Jennie had reservations. "It would be a really great party if everyone stayed to the end. Last year the high school boys kind of drifted away early, and you got the feeling that all the excitement went with them."

Maggie was looking thoughtful. "Steve, will you see that Matt meets some of your friends and has a good time this first year?" she suggested.

Matt ducked his head, embarrassed, and Steve glanced at him with a calculating look, as if Steve's mother had caused an awkward situation. But he did not annoy her by saying so.

Becky said, "My Brownie troop is going to meet at one of the campfires and we'll have our own contest about costumes. I want to be a pumpkin."

"I think a pumpkin costume would be fun to make," Maggie told her.

"Mrs. Badger says she'll walk us all home afterward. She says maybe we'll see witches flying in the moonlight!"

"I'm going to be a Sasquatch," Andy announced, grinning broadly.

"So'm I," said Tommy. "We saw the costumes in the variety store today."

When the big night came, Jennie and Liza went as witches. They took Becky in her pumpkin costume to the Brownies' campfire and then looked around for Marky's fire. The playground was swarming with Halloween figures, big and little, masked and unmasked, and there were six fires burning at different spots around the playground. The girls found Marky's fire, closest to the woods at the back of the playground. And beyond the fire, figures were moving restlessly in the dim light, wearing masks like ugly dragons and looking as if they were searching for something.

"That's Steve's crowd." Jennie pointed them out to Liza. "I can tell the bouncy way Greg Forrest walks. And Johnny Jones—he always looks mad about something, even in a mask. And Randy Gardner—he's the one with the guitar. He never goes anywhere without it."

Steve's crowd was collecting around a campfire on the farthest side of the playground. Liza recognized Matt's checked shirt. Several girls were joining the boys, and the sounds of guitar and singing came clearly across the playground.

Barney Applegate and Fred Stefansson joined the girls then, and Liza forgot about the older boys. Barney and Fred kept telling stories about ghosts and spooks that the girls had never heard before, and they were laughing most of the time—when Fred wasn't scaring them into shudders with a ghost story "that really happened." At least six Sasquatches of different sizes were moving from one fire to another. Every time Fred saw one, he remembered a new story about the Sasquatch, the Bigfoot who roams the western wilderness.

A masked gypsy came to their group on her way around the fires and told their fortunes. She looked at Liza keenly as she studied her palm in the light of the fire, and said, "You're going to lose a lot of weight this year. Just hold that thought and it will happen. Just watch it!" That prophecy made the whole evening a success for Liza.

The costume parade followed when the fires began to burn down a little, and after that the crowd began drifting away as the parade broke up. Barney said, "We'll walk with you on the way home, girls. No telling who's out tonight in these masks."

Two blocks from home they heard sirens howling. A police car came screaming down the street with its light swiveling, and Jennie stopped, with a taut expression, and watched the patrol car as it passed them. Liza could feel the tension in the air.

Barney said to Fred, "Let's see what's happening!" And then, to the girls, "You're okay now! See you in school!" And they ran after the police car.

Liza looked at Jennie. "Should we go and see what's happening?"

Jennie shook her head. "I don't want to know."

They went on home, sobered at the thought of something calling out the police, and found Becky sitting at the kitchen table drinking hot cocoa with Maggie and Don. The cookie jar was on the table, and a bowl of marshmallows for the cocoa. As the girls came in, Becky shrieked, "I got a prize! Look!" She displayed a little plastic pumpkin with a lighted candle inside.

Maggie filled cups of cocoa for them, and listened to their stories about the evening. "Did you see Steve and Matt?" she asked.

"I saw them in the beginning," Jennie said, trying to be very casual. "They were with Steve's crowd. We heard them singing—"

"You didn't see them leave?" Maggie's voice was strained, and Liza looked from Maggie to her father. The Sasquatches came home then, charged with news.

"The police were at the Nutmeg shop!" Tommy announced gleefully. "We couldn't see much. They were arresting someone, but we couldn't see him. The window was broken. And the Nutmeg lady was mad. Boy, was she mad!"

Maggie looked at Don, and he met her glance, putting his hand on hers.

The telephone rang and Liza froze. The sound was ominous at this time of night. Don answered it and came back to the table.

"I've got to go out and get Matt," he said, and left before anyone could ask any questions.

Becky was rubbing her eyes and yawning, and Maggie said, "Don't try to stay up, Becky. Go to bed and dream about your prize." Too sleepy to argue, Becky said good night to everyone and stumbled, yawning, upstairs. The Sasquatches followed within ten minutes.

Half an hour later Don came home with Matt, who looked despondent, and sagged down into a chair as if he hated the world.

"Where's Steve?" Maggie asked, setting a cup of cocoa before him. "Didn't you stay together?"

Matt took a sip of hot cocoa. "We got separated."

Maggie looked at Don, lifting her eyebrows in a question, and then turned back to Matt. "If Steve got into trouble, I've got to know, Matt. Is he in trouble?"

"Not that I know of."

Don said quietly, "We'll talk about it later."

Matt drained his cup, got up and tramped out of the kitchen and on up the back stairs. They heard his door slam hard enough to shake the wall.

"Don, what happened?" Maggie said.

He reached a hand across the table and held hers. "Matt was arrested," he said. "He won't talk about it. But as far as I can figure out what happened, he left the school grounds with some of the boys for tricks or treats, a shopwindow got broken, someone called the police. When they arrived there, Matt was the only one around, and he was arrested with a carton of pewter things in his hands."

Maggie said nothing, but her hand tightened in his. Jennie gasped and held her hand over her mouth, staring at him. Liza felt her pulse suddenly pounding. Matt? Arrested? But someone must be crazy!

"He's got a court appearance next Friday." Don shook his head. "I don't understand it! Matt was never in trouble in his life before, and here he is, getting some kind of police record. And he won't say anything about it, except that the shop owner says a lot of things were stolen and he had one of them in his hands when the police got there. Matt just says the other boys got away and he didn't. But he won't give any names. He says maybe he was a sucker to get into it, but that was his own fault."

There was a long silence. Liza got up and began putting mugs into the sink for washing.

"Something happens every Halloween," Jennie said. Liza glanced at her over her shoulder. Jennie's dark brows were drawn together as if something hurt. "Last year one of Steve's friends was arrested for vandalism—Johnny Jones. He was on probation for maybe eight months, and Steve thought nobody was being fair about it."

Maggie was sitting with her hand over her eyes, withdrawn and pained.

"Don," she said. "Do you think Steve was in this?"

He met her eyes, reached for her hand again, and said, "Maggie, I think he had to be. Matt went out with Steve's crowd. I don't think he would have joined another crowd. He doesn't know that many kids yet."

She shook her head. "I suppose so. But I can't believe it was intentional."

"Whatever happened"—Don tried to comfort her—"we'll just play it slow and easy. It'll all come out sooner or later—"

"But of course Matt can't tell on somebody else!" Liza cried.

"I'm waiting to see if any of the other boys will stand up for Matt, now he's in trouble," Don said skeptically.

"But a police record!" Liza protested. "Just for a Halloween trick?"

"But the window was broken at the Silver Nutmeg, and the owner says a lot of things were stolen. Matt was standing there with stolen goods in his hands and says he doesn't know anything about anybody else. He says he was trying to return them, but she doesn't believe him."

Maggie got up and turned toward the stairs as if she was very tired. Don joined her.

"Don't ask Matt about it," he said to the girls, "unless he wants to open up and talk to you."

Liza turned back to the sink and began washing the mugs. "That Nutmeg woman," she said. "I was in there once. She thinks everyone might be stealing from her. She hates kids—"

"I know," Jennie said. "Last spring Steve talked about how the guys hate her, about getting even with her . . ."

Liza swished the mugs through suds, thinking about Steve. And about Matt. All the possibilities were so ugly and painful that she tried to believe it was all impossible.

"Steve's been in a real trauma ever since we left Tacoma," Jennie said, as if she were talking to herself. "He was in high school then, and he hated leaving. Ever since we came here he's talked about cutting out and going it alone so he won't be a burden on Mom. And he didn't want her to marry again."

Liza heard her, feeling as if a chill wind had blown through the house. She had been hoping Steve was liking his stepfamily better, was getting along better with Matt, and now this.

But perhaps it wasn't really anything to do with Steve at all. Maybe Matt had just happened along when someone was breaking the window. Maybe he really didn't know who it was, with masks and disguises and all.

"Mom always worried about Halloween," Jennie remarked.

11

MATT'S COURT APPEARANCE was set for the following Friday, and all that week Liza could hardly face school from day to day. The only one she could talk to about Matt's trouble was Barney.

"You remember when the police sirens came screaming up the street Halloween night, and you ran back to see what was going on?" she asked him after school one day.

"Yeah, that was the deal at the Silver Nutmeg. Fred and I got there right after the police car did. Miss Kapek was yelling about how there ought to be a law about Halloween, and the police said, 'Now, lady, you don't have to get excited, we'll take care of everything.'" Liza could imagine the scene and smiled in spite of herself. "And Matt was the only guy standing there—with this carton, as if it was heavy. He said he thought he could help after—after the window got broken, and the other kids grabbed stuff and ran off."

"Did you see the other kids?"

Barney shook his head. "There was kind of a crowd because of the sirens, and I couldn't really tell what was going on . . . everybody pushing around, a couple of guys running away—only I couldn't see who they were."

"I know Matt didn't do it," Liza said tensely.

"Could have been Steve's friends," Barney said. "They were in trouble like that last year. Johnny Jones got six months' probation for something the police caught him doing."

So the week wore uneasily on to Friday, when Don took Matt to court. That night at dinner Don told the family what had happened.

"Miss Kapek said a friend who lived near the shop called her and told her something was going on there. So Miss Kapek called the police and then went to the shop. The window was smashed and Matt was the only person in sight—in the middle of the floor with this carton of pewter figures."

Matt said, "I stepped through the window when the glass was gone. Someone let go of that carton, and I was going to return it—"

"So then Miss Kapek said when she checked the stockroom the next morning that the back door had been opened and several boxes of crystal and silver were gone." Don continued the story. "She says about five hundred dollars' worth of damage was done—and stolen."

"I didn't know anything about that," Matt said, as if he was tired of repeating himself.

His dad said, "Matt, we aren't worried about what you were doing that night. We believe exactly what you say. But other boys were there part of the time, and you knew them, didn't you?" He looked at his son with a probing stare, and Matt dropped his eyes.

"Matt!" Don said sharply, and the boy's head came up. "You will answer my question, yes or no! I'm not asking who they were. I'm saying that you did know the boys who smashed the window. Didn't you?"

"Yeah. I guess so."

"Okay. The point is, if you're going to protect them, then you will have to pay for the damage they did. There's no other way out. If you take that kind of responsibility, you take it all the way."

"Okay." Matt sounded bored, as if he had heard it all before. "I can get a job. I can pay it off."

"Gee!" breathed Tommy, looking from Don to Matt across the table. "You mean, Matt's going to pay all that money, himself?"

"Somebody's got to pay it," Don said. "And if Matt wants to take the blame for something he didn't do, I guess he'll have to pay for it."

"Gee!" Tommy said again. "You mean you could turn somebody in and you're not going to?"

He was incredulous in his admiration. Liza glanced at Steve. He looked self-conscious and unhappy. Matt was red with embarrassment. "Oh, for Pete's sake! Let's forget it, Dad. The court gave me plenty of time—I mean, a year to pay off in—it's no big deal. Why keep it going?"

"I don't see why anyone should have to pay for something he didn't do," Jennie protested. "That isn't fair, either."

Don said, "If we knew who did it, Matt wouldn't have to pay. But the way it stands now, he's the one who's tagged with the bill. But when someone in this family is in trouble, it affects all of us. Matt won't have to cope with this alone."

Liza looked at Steve and saw in his eyes a strange recognition of her as a person, not admiring, not impressed, but puzzled. And she saw him for the first time, not as a star personality, but as a real person touching or not touching a brother's trouble . . . and she thought, what kind of boy is he, after all? Will he offer to help?

The heavy atmosphere overhanging the table lightened and Don looked around at the family. "All right," he said on a note of relief. "I hope this is the last time we'll have to talk about Halloween. Now, tomorrow morning we start work on the boys' bathroom. That's the last job to be done on the house, and we want it finished before Thanksgiving, so we can really celebrate the season. Matt and Steve will work with me, and it ought to go fairly fast."

"I've got a football game in the afternoon," Matt said.

"You can work in the morning," Don answered. "Steve and I can do a lot in the afternoon."

"But I've got plans for tomorrow," Steve said. "Busy all day—"

"Something important? Like a job?"

"Well, yeah. Anyway, important." Steve sounded defensive.

"That's good news, Steve. Tell me about it. The marina?"

Steve shook his head. "This is something else," he said, as if he would rather not talk about it. "I don't know that they'd want me to talk about it. But the guys have got something going, and I promised to help, and they said to be sure not to let them down."

"The guys?" Don asked. "The ones who were with you Halloween night?"

"Well, it's our crowd," Steve said warily. "They're my friends, Don. So what's wrong with helping friends do a job?"

"Nothing's wrong with helping friends on a job," Don said. "But on my job tomorrow I need your help a lot more than your friends do. You can call them tonight and explain."

He held Steve's eyes for a moment, and Steve said, "Well, okay, then. I'll tell them when I see them tonight."

"Better call them, Steve. I want you in the shop tonight. We're going to work on pipe fittings and get the outlines of this bathroom job in hand. It's going to take a couple of hours every night and all day Saturdays and Sundays to get it finished before Thanksgiving."

Steve scowled blackly, and then, throwing his napkin on the table, he stood up and spat out an obscenity. As he turned to go, Don jumped to his feet and grabbed the boy's shoulders with hard fingers Steve could not shake off.

"The next time I hear you use language like that in this house, I'll break your jaw! Do you understand? We don't use that kind of language in this family, and you will apologize at once."

Liza stared, appalled that her father should treat Steve like a small boy. Then to her amazement, Steve said, "Sorry, Mom! It got out because I was so mad." Then, with a theatrical air, he bowed to Liza, sweeping an imaginary hat, and to Jennie and to Becky, and said, "My apologies, ladies!" and bowed again as if he were accepting applause.

Don watched him with exasperation. But he sat down at his place and said, "All right, Steve. Now put in your call."

Steve shrugged and went to the phone in the kitchen. They could hear him saying, "So I got trapped into some repair job around the house here. No way out—" When he returned to the table, he was sullen again.

"It's your bathroom, you know," Don reminded him. "It's a matter of carrying your weight around here."

Steve stared at Don as if he challenged his stepfather to a duel of authority, and Don stared him down. Steve dropped his eyes and said no more. But he spent the evening with Matt and Don in the workshop.

The work on the bathroom went forward after that with no further friction. Matt played football on Saturday afternoons, and Steve worked alone with Don. Oddly, he seemed less sullen, and even interested in the skills he was learning.

At dinner one night Don said, "Steve is doing a really great job for me. I told him he could be a rich man if he just put his mind to being a plumber!"

Steve looked pained at the conversation, but a secret satisfaction showed through. And when the family inspected the finished bathroom on Thanksgiving morning, Steve showed them details of the work with as much pride as Don himself.

The bath was all new, with fiberglass tub enclosure, wide mirrors above the marble counter with double sinks and two medicine chests, as well as cupboards below the counter. The walls were covered with vinyl paper in brown stripes.

Matt looked at everything as critically as if he had never worked on this job.

"It's okay," he said. And then, "It's *okay!*"

Steve said nothing, but he handled the mirrored doors and studied the paper on the walls with pride.

"Steve did those walls," Don said. "That paper is very tricky to hang, and he did a superior job. I'm thinking of putting him on the payroll."

In spite of careful indifference, Steve's secret pleasure in Don's approval showed through. He smiled at Liza for the first time she could remember, and, startled, she wondered if it was only an accident. But somehow she was feeling optimistic these days. As if things were going better than she had hoped, and as if Steve was—well, joining the family.

And then she remembered suddenly that Matt had said several weeks ago that she was looking thinner. Somehow she could not really believe that. But still . . . Steve *had* smiled at her.

She went to her own room, locked the door,

stripped off her clothes, and stepped on the scale.

One hundred and forty-five pounds! She was incredulous. Fifteen pounds lighter! How could that have happened? She looked at herself in the mirror and thought her face looked thinner. She looked into her eyes in the mirror and said aloud, awestruck, "I'm not even hungry!"

She dressed again, trying on a pair of slacks she had not worn for a year, and found they fitted. She went down to Thanksgiving dinner in a state of euphoria.

The table was decorated with favors at each place and a centerpiece of wild rose hips and snowberries with golden bracken. It was the prettiest table Liza had ever seen. The last Thanksgiving dinner . . . she didn't want to remember.

Don ate his flaky croissant roll and said, "Wow! I never knew I was getting a gourmet cook, with all your other virtues!" He got up from his place, went to the other end of the table, and kissed Maggie's hand. "My salute to the chef!"

Steve was watching Don as if he was not sure whether to be pleased or not, but his eyes softened as he looked at his mother's face.

Then he said, "Mom, you scored again! You do make holidays worthwhile!"

"Thanks, Steve." Maggie sounded touched. "I don't know whether I'm getting better or you are."

"It's a draw," Don said. "We're a different family from last August."

Liza thought about last August. Maybe they

were different. She would like to believe it. With a sigh she ate two bites of pumpkin pie and laid down her fork.

Maggie's pie was better than any Liza had ever tasted. But today she wasn't hungry. Really.

12

THE DAY AFTER THANKSGIVING was the first day of Christmas shopping, the day that Santa Claus came to town, the day all the Christmas lights went on. Liza looked forward to Christmas shopping this year all the more, because last year had been too sad for Christmas. She was in the shopping district by nine thirty Friday morning.

She looked first in the variety store for toys and games for Becky and the two younger boys and found nothing there. She hesitated at the corner by the Silver Nutmeg and decided, after all, not to shop there again. She remembered another gift shop at the far end of Main Street and rode out to the Magic Lantern, where she found a pretty decorated mirror for Becky.

By the time she got back to Applegate's to look for something for Andy and Tommy, it was going on eleven o'clock. She wedged through the crowd around the candy counter and the greeting cards, to the toys and games, where she looked at puzzles, and could not decide between three of them.

Mrs. Applegate smiled at her. "Seems hardly

possible it's Christmas again," she said. "Why, it was summer just the day before yesterday. Can I help you with anything?"

"Thanks, I just want to look around a little."

Mrs. Applegate nodded and moved down the aisle to help another customer with perfumes. Liza picked out a dinosaur puzzle and another about spacemen on the moon, exhilarated with so many successes in one morning. She turned into a long aisle lined with toys and coloring books.

A couple of women were selecting scrapbooks and coloring pens, and beyond them Steve was looking at gift pen-and-pencil sets. Liza was about to hail him when she remembered that he didn't much like her to act friendly in public. She stopped beside another customer and looked at a coloring book with detailed drawings of medieval princesses and knights, wondering if she should add it to her present for Becky. Then she looked through another with wild animals roaming tropical forests, glancing at Steve now and then, wondering for whom he was buying a pen and pencil set. Dad perhaps?

The other customer moved away, and suddenly Liza froze. Turning his back slightly, Steve put four boxes of ten-dollar pen and pencil sets into his pocket as casually as if he were reaching for a handkerchief.

Liza let out a gasp and then suppressed it, moving along the aisle away from him, trying to think what she ought to do. She could not let him get away with stealing forty dollars' worth of merchandise from the Applegates. And yet she could not tell him here in public that she had seen him take that merchandise.

She moved over to the cash register, where Barney was ringing up several items for a customer with a string shopping bag. Liza stood behind her, looking into the mirror designed to watch customers. Steve was leaving the store by another door without approaching the cash register. She looked around. Mrs. Applegate was rearranging bottles on the shelves behind the perfume counter. Mr. Applegate was looking out of the pharmacy department at the back of the store, and he waved to Liza. She waved back and then moved up to the cash register. Barney rang up her purchases, and she paid him.

"Barney," she said, very low. "Can you get away? I've got to talk to you."

"Gee, I don't know." He looked across the store at the clock. It was going on twelve. "Mom? Can I get some lunch while we're not busy?"

Liza was hot with embarrassment. His mom called over her shoulder, "Go ahead, Barney. I'll take the cash register while you're gone. I left things for sandwiches on the counter in the kitchen. Can you be back in half an hour?"

He closed the cash register and walked out with Liza, saying, "Wanta come home with me for lunch? I haven't got much time off today."

"I guess so." Walking her bike, she said, "Barney, the most awful thing happened while I was in your store. I saw someone shoplifting!"

He stared at her. "Why didn't you tell somebody right then?"

"I couldn't. I just couldn't. It was Steve." She was shaking with tension now that it was out.

"Steve? Steve Duncan? You're kidding!"

"No, I'm not. I wish I were!" She shook her head. She could feel tears getting ready to embarrass her. She shook her head again to get rid of them. "He didn't see me, but I was looking at the coloring books and he was down there where the pens and pencils are, and the next thing he put four sets in his pocket. Like nothing. Like packages of gum! And then he walked out. I couldn't say anything then, Barney. But I thought you might know how to handle it."

"How do you mean, handle it?" He sounded mad.

"I mean, there's got to be some mistake. I can't believe Steve would steal. But I saw him! Oh, Barney, I feel terrible. And I don't want Maggie to know. Or Dad. Why would Steve do something like that?"

"Or how often has he stolen something before?" Barney sounded cynical. "We'd better try to find him. Talk to him. Anyone else, I'd call the police. But so long as it's your family, Liza—Okay, we'll try to figure it out some other way."

"I don't want your father to know about it, either," she said. "I'd be so embarrassed! I'm so ashamed of Steve now, and I feel terrible about it!" Then she did break down and cry with long gasping sobs, and people looked at her, wondering what was wrong. Barney steered her toward the corner.

"Isn't that Steve coming out of Atwater's hardware?"

105

She looked where he was pointing, half a block away, and it was indeed Steve. Her heart began to thump so hard she was gasping again, and Barney said, "Come on, we'll catch up with him and settle this right now."

She didn't want to. She couldn't bear for Steve to know she had told on him.

"Hey, Steve!" Barney yelled. "Wait up, will ya?"

Steve hesitated as if his first impulse was to start running. But he waited for Barney and Liza to catch up with him, smiling a little with that special handsome arrogance that hit Liza with fresh impact. It was more unfriendly than she expected.

"Hi, kids! What's on your mind, Barney?"

Barney glanced around. "Gotta talk to you, Steve. Come on around to my house, we can't talk on the street."

"I'm kinda busy today, Barney. Make it another time, will you?"

Barney shook his head. "It's gotta be now. And if you want it here on the street, that's how it will be. Only I thought it might be better if we could talk it over privately."

Steve glared at Liza and she wilted. "Barney," she said miserably, "maybe I should go on home and let Maggie know I'm all right."

"You wanta tell Maggie, you mean?"

Liza wanted to sag down on the ground and disappear.

"Tell Mom what?" Steve demanded. And, oddly, he was looking scared.

"Okay," Barney said. "I can't stand here arguing all day. You took some pen and pencil sets from my dad's store, and I want to know why."

"Oh, if that's all! You don't understand. It's a game, that's all. A test of skill. You gotta be quick in this game. And then return them later."

Barney looked skeptical. "I'll take them now."

Steve said, "A couple of ballpoint pens isn't going to break your dad! What's the big deal, anyway?"

"Anyone else, I'd call the police," Barney said. "Stealing is something you go to jail for. Hadn't you heard?"

"Aw, don't be ridiculous! I guess I flunked the test of skill, that's all. So I got seen! Here's your merchandise if you want to be cheap about it!" He pulled out the four small packages and stuffed them into Barney's jacket. "Now forget about it. Okay?"

"No, it's not okay," Barney said. Liza was watching Steve's face, wanting to believe him, glad he gave up his loot so easily, and yet—and yet—there was still something terribly wrong. Barney went on. "How do I know you haven't got a lot more stuff stashed away somewhere? We've been missing things right along."

A quick flicker in Steve's eyes gave him away. He did have loot stashed away. She knew as if she had seen it printed in capitals.

"What did you bring out of the hardware store?" Barney asked.

"Nothing." But his tone was not convincing.

"Oh, Steve," Liza said. "I feel so bad about all

this. I don't want anything to happen to you. I don't want Maggie to get hurt."

"So you're the one who turned me in!" He looked at her with contempt, and she felt as if she were the guilty one. "I might have known a girl wouldn't have any sense of loyalty."

Suddenly Liza's patience snapped and all her illusions disappeared like mist in the sun, leaving her as angry as he was.

"Loyalty to what?" she cried. "When I see someone stealing something I'm going to report it, and when I think my stepbrother is going to be a crook, I think he should be stopped. I thought you were so great, once, and now I wish I never had to see you again!"

"Oh, for crying out loud!" Steve protested. "I never heard so much noise about such a nothing! I gave the stuff back to you, Barney. I told you it was just a game! Now for Pete's sake, let's just forget the whole deal. And don't say anything to Mom!"

"You are a fake," Liza said very distinctly. "I can't stand fakes!"

She turned her back and said to Barney, "Let's go get your lunch and figure out where we go from here."

In Barney's kitchen they made peanut butter sandwiches and drank homemade milkshakes. "Maybe I ought to talk to Matt," Liza said. "I don't think it's something to forget."

Barney shook his head and tossed a crumb of sandwich to Cockeyed Sam, who caught it in midair. "Now that you mention Matt," he said, "Steve and his gang were with him on Halloween night. Maybe you should tell your dad about this business today."

She shook her head. "Not Dad! He'd be terribly upset. And so would Maggie. But maybe Matt could get to Steve."

13

ALL LIZA WANTED NOW was to get home and try to sort out all the grief and anger that assailed her. She rode back wondering how she was going to act. What was she going to say? What was she going to hear when she got home? What might have happened since she last saw Steve? How was he going to act? Her heart kept beating fast and hard, as if danger threatened.

She slipped into the house at two in the afternoon, went up to her all-alone place and settled in the chimney corner. Wrapped in a warm blanket, she looked out at the sky with its golden streaks of sunlight above the quiet waters of the sound. She let herself float in the solitude of the skies, separated from world and trouble. Gradually she found herself quieting, thinking this trouble had to be straightened out before Christmas, but she was not alone with it.

She got up and went downstairs to Matt's room. He was at his desk, resting his head on one hand while he wrote a paper. He paid no attention to the door's opening, and Liza hesitated about interrupting him. But this was something that could not wait.

110

"Matt, can I talk to you a minute?"

"Why now?" He sounded irritated. "I'm just into this paper."

"But this is real trouble, Matt. I've got to talk to someone."

"Okay, okay." He turned to face Liza, sitting on the edge of the bed.

"It's about Steve."

Matt came to attention. "What's he been doing now?"

"Well, I saw him shoplifting in Applegate's pharmacy this morning." Matt was staring at her intently. "I told Barney about it. And we followed him up the street. He gave Barney back the pen and pencil sets he had taken. But he said it was just some kind of game! The Mariners told him to do it to be a member. So what if he does it again? Do I have to tell Dad? And I keep thinking how bad Maggie would feel. What should we do?"

Matt shook his head. "I can't figure the guy. And that bunch he goes with—they're all into this kind of thing."

She caught her breath. "But, Matt! If you know about his friends, maybe you should say something to Dad. What if they get Steve into big trouble?"

"I can't go finking to Dad about stories I hear at the high school!" Matt said impatiently, as if anyone should know that. "And if those kids are getting him into trouble, well, it's Steve's choice. Why don't you tell Maggie and Dad what you saw Steve doing today?"

Why didn't she?

But you just didn't go telling adults on another kid. Besides, what if her dad got so tough, he turned Steve off altogether? What if Steve couldn't take it and ran away?

"But why Steve?" she wondered aloud. "I mean, he acted as if he was liking this family better at Thanksgiving."

Matt shook his head. "Steve is eaten up inside about his old man. He told me once his dad ran off to South America. Steve said something about embezzling half a million dollars." Matt shook his head. "He tried to think it wasn't so bad. I can see how a guy would feel about a father like that—you'd be hoping to find out something good about him!" Then—"Does Jennie know about this today?"

"I haven't told her. Haven't seen her yet."

She found Jennie watching television with the younger children. The show would be over in five minutes, and Liza waited. Then, "Can you come upstairs, Jennie? Matt wants to talk to you."

Jennie followed her up to Matt's room.

"What's wrong now?" Jennie asked, looking from Liza to Matt, who was sitting at his desk, staring at a picture on the wall as if he were studying it for answers. It was a picture of a mountain man wrestling with a mountain lion.

Matt said, "Liza, you tell Jennie about this morning."

Jennie listened to Liza's report without surprise.

"I'd hoped he wasn't going to do that anymore," she said, as if she had hoped for too much.

112

Liza stared at her. "Has he done this before?"

Jennie nodded. "The first I knew about it was a year ago, when a friend told me she saw Steve stealing in the dime store. I told him I heard about it and that I thought stealing was terrible, and he said a couple of dollars wouldn't break any storekeeper. So I said that it wasn't honest, and Steve said"—she stopped a moment—"Steve said, 'What's honesty got to do with anything these days?'"

Matt looked up. "I suppose after his father's running out—and he said something about embezzlement?"

Jennie nodded. "Dad was the vice-president of the top bank in Tacoma, and he stole half a million dollars and got it out to Brazil, and when they found out about it, he ran out—got away. He's been in Brazil ever since." She blew her nose and wiped her eyes. "You don't know what it's like to read things like that about your father in the headline of the morning paper! We couldn't go to school that day— we couldn't bear to face anyone. And after that there wasn't any money and Mom had to look for a job right away. There aren't very many jobs when you need them. She finally got this job in Avalon, and she hoped that maybe here people wouldn't know we were the Duncans who had been in the paper. And Steve took it the hardest of all. He was pretty close to our dad, and we'd just had this great trip on our boat, cruising up the Inland Passage to Alaska. That was in July. Steve was crazy about Alaska. He wanted to stay there. And then in September, Dad was gone. And we had to sell the boat, of course. Only we didn't have any money left anyway—there were so many bills, Mom said."

She sat there, holding her hand over her eyes, and Liza felt as if this was her own tragedy. So that was what Dad had meant, when he said the Duncans had been through trouble.

"And then, when you think about your dad being a criminal," Jennie went on, "you wonder if you inherited that—being a criminal, I mean. Like alcoholism. Steve says he doesn't want to be like Dad. But what if he can't help it?"

Matt said, "I don't think you inherit anything like—well, stealing."

Jennie said, "I keep saying that. But sometimes I wonder."

Liza said, "But what should we do, Jennie?"

Jennie shook her head again. "I don't know. I just don't know. I talked to Mom the other time, and she talked to our pastor, and he talked to Steve, and the school counselor talked to him. But nothing really got through. All I know, he's not happy about anything. And I don't know what anyone can do about that, either."

Then she smiled faintly, hopefully. "I think maybe if Don knew about it, he'd know what to do. But I couldn't go and tell him."

Matt shook his head. "Not right now, I couldn't either. But he'll find out. It just happens that way."

14

THE NEXT WEEK the school was busy with preparations for the Christmas program, to be produced
some two weeks later. Jennie was singing in the cho-
rus, Matt was one of the three kings in the pageant.
Steve was working at the marina, very busy with
preparations for the Christmas party there, a high-
light of the year.

Liza saw him walking with Kim in the halls, as
usual, talking as if they were making great plans. In
school he acted as if he didn't know Liza, also as
usual.

When she came home the first Monday in De-
cember, she saw a letter on the hall table for Steve.
And then she saw it was postmarked from Brazil. Her
pulsebeat jumped with suspense. It must be from
Steve's father.

Steve was late getting home from the marina
that night. He arrived just as the family was ready to
sit down at the table. Maggie was putting dressing on
the tossed salad in the big bowl, adding hard-boiled
eggs and olives at the last minute. Liza was pouring
milk in the glasses on the table when she heard Steve

come in, bang the door behind him, hesitate a moment, and then tear upstairs with hard, impatient two-at-a-time steps.

"Now that Steve's home, we'll wait a minute for him," Maggie said.

A few minutes later she rang the dinner bell, and the family gathered in the dining room. Steve was the last to arrive, and when he did, he entered the dining room with a stiff and jaunty air, whistling through his teeth as if he were suppressing some kind of frustration.

Jennie talked about the decorations the art elective class was making for the Christmas programs: huge gold-foil stars in different sizes. "The teacher says everyone who works in the class can make a star to bring home," she said.

Maggie said, "That will be lovely, Jennie." And then, "Steve, I saw you had a letter from your father. What's the news from Rio?"

"He said, 'Don't come down here!'" Steve's mouth twisted. "So that's out!" He flung down his napkin and got to his feet in a painful gesture of rejection. "So where do I go now, when my own father doesn't even want to see me?"

He left the room and they heard him tramping heavily upstairs, and then down again, and he called back from the front hall, "I'll be out with the guys!"

The door slammed behind him.

Tommy listened thoughtfully, and then said, "I wish we could see Daddy again! Remember that time he took us on that long boat trip that summer? He was lots of fun."

116

Maggie reached out her hand to Tommy.

"We're all sorry Daddy went away," she said. And then she looked at Don with an expression of fear and grief.

"I don't know what to do about it!" she said. "Steve keeps trying to reach his father. And he feels so rejected and so bitter—"

"Maggie, all we can do now is to give him support," Don said. "He's got to find his own way, somehow. And the will to survive. A parent can only take a boy so far—"

She sat there, staring out of the window. "But he's failing in school . . . there's got to be some kind of answer, Don. What should we be doing?"

Don shook his head. "He's got to figure it out," he said. "I've been asking him about it. He talks about going to Alaska. Or going to sea. And he might be better off away from home. And away from those friends he runs with."

"You mean, when he graduates?"

"Whenever the time is right," Don said. "Maybe he should learn more about real life even before he finishes school."

Liza caught Jennie's eye and realized they were both thinking the same thing: Don must know more about Steve's adventures than they had thought. Maggie looked far away through the window, silently. And Liza and Jennie got up to clear the table.

When Liza brought the coffee in some minutes later, Don was saying, "Steve needs a man's point of view. Of course he's had a bad time—after his father ran out on him. But so did you have a bad time. He's got to learn to cope instead of feeling sorry for himself." He got up and went to her end of the table. "Come on, honey," he said. He took her hands and drew her up from her chair. "We'll take the coffee out to the TV room and see that program you wanted to see, about eagles."

She smiled at him wanly and they went out to the TV room, while Jennie and Liza cleaned up the kitchen.

"Dad doesn't like Steve's friends," Liza remarked. "I thought they were supposed to be the top boys in the senior class, being the Mariners, and everything."

"I never liked them," Jennie said flatly. "A couple of them used to come over last year and they were always kidding around about ways to raise money, like stealing here and there. And they talked about getting a couple of thousand together by the time they were graduating, so they could charter a boat and go up to Alaska."

"When did he begin going with Kim?" Liza wanted to know.

"Oh, that was last spring. He'd go over to her house to study two or three nights a week. I don't know how much Kim knew about that bunch, but he acted last summer as if he thought she was kind of bossy, trying to make him work harder in English, and read more books . . . even trying to keep him away from his crowd."

"Maybe that was a good idea."

"Oh, all her ideas were good. Only, this fall Steve began resisting. I heard him tell her once it wasn't going to work out, as if he wanted to break up with her. But there wasn't any other girl, so they kind of kept it going."

The telephone rang and Liza picked it up. It was for her dad. She opened the TV room door. "Telephone for you, Dad." As he got up from his chair, she said, "I think it's trouble."

Don picked up the telephone in the kitchen. "Thank you, officer. I'll be right there."

Maggie came out of the TV room, and he said, "The police have arrested Steve."

Maggie's hand flew to her mouth.

"Funny thing," Don said. "It was the Silver Nutmeg again. That place must be a jinx."

"I'll go with you," said Maggie.

They rushed out. The girls heard the car doors slam and the motor revving up. They looked at each other.

Jennie shook her head. "This does it! And I guess it's a good thing for Mom and Don to know all about it now."

Liza found herself shaking. She had to keep a tight grip on herself not to set a glass down too hard, not to drop a plate as she put it on the stack in the cupboard. She wished she could talk to Barney. But this had nothing to do with him.

She and Jennie finished the dishes and then sat down and stared at the TV screen until their parents returned. When Liza heard the car come into the drive, she could not recall anything she had seen on TV. She shut off the set and went into the kitchen as Maggie and Don came in the back door. Behind them, Steve went up the back stairs, slowly and heavily.

Maggie and Don came into the kitchen, sat down wearily at the table, and looked at the girls, who sat down with them.

"What happened?" Jennie asked in a hushed voice.

"Steve and Johnny Jones were fooling around in the Silver Nutmeg," Don said. "Miss Kapek is pretty suspicious about kids in the shop these days. She watched them and saw they were putting things into their pockets. She called the police. When the police got there they searched the boys and found the stuff." He sighed and rubbed his forehead as if he was very tired. "So we've got to go to court again. Week from Wednesday. Steve didn't want to talk about it on the way home, but there was nothing to say. It's an open-and-shut case of shoplifting."

"I felt kind of sorry for Johnny Jones," Maggie said. "His folks wouldn't even come to the station. They said to let him spend the night there. It might be good for him."

Don looked at her and grinned a little. "That might be true. From what I hear around town, they've been through this before." Then, "Don't badger Steve with questions about this thing. He won't want to talk. And I'm going to have him working with me from now on."

For the next week, Don kept Steve busy in the shop after school and in the evenings, learning about electrical connections, repairs on small appliances, fixing lamp switches, rewiring lamps. Steve seemed reasonably interested in what he was learning and acted as if he had forgotten the court hearing.

At dinner one night Don said, as if they had talked about it before, "What's the attraction about Alaska, Steve? Tell me more about it."

"It sounds like the other side of the frontier," Steve said, with an enthusiasm Liza had not seen him show over anything else. "It's like starting where the world is just beginning—next best thing to being on a boat."

"Do you think of staying there? Working? Or just visiting?"

"Who knows?" Steve shrugged, and his eyes looked into some faraway dream. "If I found a job, I might stay there forever. There's nothing else I'm all that keen about doing. And up there I might find what I'm looking for."

"Like gold?" Tommy was bright-eyed.

Steve grinned at his little brother and shoved his hand over Tommy's face as if he were wiping off the wisecracking grin.

"Maybe peace," he said. "Maybe I'll find out where I'm going. And why."

The table was silent for a moment, and Liza thought about Steve's words. They revealed a hunger and uncertainty she had never suspected.

"That's about as good a reason as any for exploration," Don said. "There ought to be some right way to go about it. How do you plan to get there, Steve? What about money?"

Steve looked momentarily adrift. "That's the

problem. How do I know? Maybe I could get some kind of job that would take me in that direction. Maybe I could hitch on some boat."

Andy looked at the clock and cried, "Say, there's a documentary on Alaska right now! About the early gold-rush days!"

"I'll watch it with you," Steve said. He rarely cared to watch any program the younger boys were interested in. Now they all trooped into the TV room, carrying ice cream to eat before the set.

An hour later the program ended and Tommy and Andy burst through the kitchen and up the back stairs, enacting a wild scene from gold-rush days. Steve, grinning at their excitement, sat down at the table to have another helping of ice cream. Liza and Jennie joined him.

"That's a great documentary," he said. "I've seen it before, but it's always good to see. That Dawson trail! And crossing the Yukon Territory! You wouldn't believe what it took to get to those gold-fields." His eyes shone.

Shots sounded from upstairs. The three in the kitchen stared at each other, jerked to attention, then rushed upstairs.

In Andy's room the boys were firing cap guns at each other, hiding behind the bed, ducking from the fire, and pretending to fall mortally wounded to the floor. Don arrived at the door with Maggie behind him just as Steve and the girls got there.

"What's going on here?" Don demanded.

The boys scrambled up from the floor in fits of giggles.

"We're practicing for New Year's Eve," Andy said, shooting another cap at Tommy, who pretended to be hit in the heart.

"Wait a minute," Don said. "Where did you get the guns?"

Both boys looked at the cap pistols as if they were surprised to find them in their hands, and grinned at Don.

"They're just cap pistols," Andy told his father. "We got them at Sampson's variety store. We're going to blow up the town at midnight on New Year's Eve."

Maggie took Tommy by the shoulder in a firm grip. "Where did you get the money?"

"You don't need money for a rip-off." Tommy aimed carefully at the cord on the window shade and shot.

"That's enough shooting!" Don said. "Drop your guns and come over here."

They eyed him warily, dropped the guns, and came over to stand before him.

"Tell me about this rip-off," he said.

"Oh, it's a game, Dad," Andy said.

"How do you play it?"

Tommy said eagerly, "You don't let anyone see you, and you get a score if you see someone else. Like I saw Steve rip off a boat magazine last summer."

Liza looked at Steve, who was white and angry and very still.

"So?" said Don. "Exactly how do you play the rip-off game, Andy? You tell me."

"Well—" Andy suddenly flushed with confusion

123

and managed not to look at his father. "You go into a store and look around, and then you pick up something and rip it off. That's all."

"But how do you rip it off?" Don persisted.

Tommy volunteered, "You get out of the store with it without anyone seeing."

"So you're stealing."

There was a sudden hush. Then Andy cried, "No, it's not stealing! It's just ripping off! All the guys do it!"

"Now let me get this straight," Don said. "You took the cap guns without paying for them. So you stole them."

"But that's what Steve does! So what's wrong with it?"

Maggie cried, "Tommy! You know better than that! You know that your dad ran away because he was stealing, just so he wouldn't have to go to prison! This is no different. Stealing is stealing."

Don reached out for her to join him, and she stood beside him, clinging to his hand.

"Okay, boys," Don said. "No matter what Steve does or what you call it, there is no game about stealing and nothing to laugh at. It hurts other people, so it's wrong. Now, Andy, you tell me how you got those guns, and don't say 'rip-off.' "

"Well, I—we—" Andy gulped and looked at the floor, then at the light in the hall outside the door, and took a deep breath. "Okay, I guess we stole them."

"Tommy, how do you say it?"

Tommy grinned impudently. "I still say we

124

ripped them off, but I guess maybe we stole them."

Don looked at him without a glimmer of smile. "You mean hurting Mr. Sampson is a funny joke?"

Tommy flushed. "No. I guess it's no joke."

"All right. So you've got a couple of cap guns that belong to Mr. Sampson. What are you going to do with them?"

"You mean pay for them? But I haven't got two bucks."

"All right, so you can't pay for them. What can you do?"

There was a long silence. Then Tommy drew a deep sigh and said, "Okay. I guess we gotta take them back to Mr. Sampson's store."

"Right," said Don. "And there's more to it than that. You've got to hand them to Mr. Sampson yourselves and explain why you are bringing them back."

"You mean, tell him we stole them, when he doesn't even know it?"

Tommy sounded as if he couldn't believe such reasoning.

"Right!" said Don. "The first thing after school tomorrow. I'll go with you."

They looked at each other sheepishly, and Liza looked at Steve. She knew, with a sense of loss, that Steve was not wonderful anymore.

He looked up and caught Liza's eyes fixed on him. For the first time she didn't look away. She didn't care what he thought. She was only trying to figure out why he acted the way he did, and why her feeling for him had disappeared. Was this the boy she had thought she was in love with all these months?

125

And how could that breathless, heart-pounding feeling have gone so completely?

She wondered if Kim knew this side of Steve. She felt almost sure Kim did not know.

Don said, "And in the meantime, Steve, before the hearing, I want you working with me next week. There's a lot of repair work in the shop and I'm falling behind."

"Okay." Steve turned and went out of the room, and Liza heard him close the door to his own room quietly. That registered somewhere in the back of her mind as a hopeful sign.

Maggie said, "Don, I think Tommy and Andy should go to court with Steve for that hearing."

The two boys looked at each other and then at their parents, chins up, not letting fear show.

Don nodded. "We'll all go to court together."

15

ON WEDNESDAY, ten days later, Don and Maggie took the boys to court. Liza felt as if she could hardly get through the day at school. Steve's absence seemed to show up like a headline, and when he was not in the corridor where she passed him every morning at ten, she felt as if every student who knew him was looking at her curiously. She sensed a feeling in the air that everybody knew where Steve was that day, and why. Liza suffered as if she herself might be to blame, as if his being a thief had rubbed off on the whole family.

When she met Marky and the other girls at lunch as usual, she tried to listen to their chatter about the Christmas programs at school, at the church, at the community clubs, and who was going to all of them. But she didn't feel like talking about Christmas parties, nor did she feel much like eating. She told the girls she had to finish up an assignment before her first afternoon class and escaped from the cafeteria.

At the end of the day, when she was getting her jacket from her locker, Kim Brown came past and stopped. "Hi, Liza! Is Steve around? I haven't seen him today."

Liza shook her head, grasping wildly for excuses. "He's not here today. He—well—he had an appointment."

"Oh." Kim sounded dissatisfied and Liza tried to think of something to divert her. "Is he all right, Liza?" Kim went on, "You know he used to call every night, and lately . . . Well, anyway, I haven't heard from him for days. When I see him I keep asking if anything's wrong, and he always says everything is okay. But I worry about him."

"I wouldn't know," said Liza. "He never talks to me."

"Well, maybe I'll call him tonight," Kim said uncertainly.

When Liza got home the house was silent. She went through to the kitchen and found Jennie working on a dessert for supper.

"Any news?" she asked, looking toward the dining room.

"Mom and Don and Steve are upstairs. They were there when I got home. The boys are out in the TV room with Becky."

"Did Dad say anything?" Liza was almost afraid to hear the bad news.

Jennie shrugged. "Mom said we'd all hear about it tonight," she said. "I guess Tommy and Andy were pretty scared." She checked the pots on the stove. "I told Mom I'd get supper tonight. I knew she'd be upset when she got home."

Liza set the table in the dining room, then sat down at the kitchen table and told Jennie about Kim's concern. The dinner was cooked, and Jennie dished it into the serving dishes. It was going on seven.

"Everything is ready," she said. "Want to ring the bell?"

Liza rang the bell at the foot of the stairs, while Jennie carried the serving dishes in to the table.

Maggie came down first, looking drawn and pale.

"Dinner looks lovely," she said, as she looked at the table. Andy and Tommy came in with Becky, very sober, and took their places without a giggle.

Don sat down at the head of the table, and Steve slipped around and sat down next to his mother. She reached out for his hand, and for Matt's, and said, "This is a good night to say our family blessing together."

They raised the circle of joined hands around the table and Maggie, smiling down the table at Don, said, "Let us always remember that we care for one another, one for all and all for one. God's grace be with us all."

Some tension seemed to have softened and subtly the atmosphere changed, as if late sunlight had come into the room. Liza, sitting at her father's left, looked across the table at Steve, and to her amazement he was looking at her. When she caught his eyes he almost smiled.

But no one, after all, wanted to talk much. Steve said, after his first bite of food, "Good chow, Jennie!"

129

and managed to smile at his sister. Jennie tried to talk about the Christmas program at the high school in another week, but somehow each person was occupied enough with his own sober thought so that talk lagged sadly down to silence.

At last dessert was finished, with nobody as hungry as usual, and the table was cleared. Don leaned forward and looked from one to another.

"Maggie and I have some very serious business to talk over with all of you," he said. "We want you to know about the court hearing today."

Steve slumped back in his chair, bored and self-conscious.

"Steve was released in my custody," Don said. "He told the judge what happened on Halloween night, and the Nutmeg stolen goods have been returned and accounted for. So Matt is cleared of those charges."

He leaned back and looked around to be sure he had everyone's attention. "The next question is how Steve is going to work out his problem. We've been talking about this, but I think it's a good thing for all of you to understand the details." He looked at Matt, and at Tommy and Andy, who flushed red and dropped their eyes. "Whatever Steve decides to do, we're all going to be affected one way or another, and you should all know the reasoning that goes into Steve's choice. Because it's going to be his decision."

He looked around the table again. "Of course, Maggie and I would like nothing better than for Steve to make up his failed courses and graduate from high school. He would have to work with me when he wasn't studying, and I'd pay an apprentice wage for the work he does." He looked at Steve as if he were repeating an earlier argument. "You'd learn a lot of useful skills. And you'd have money in the bank."

Steve was shaking his head slowly. "No way!" he said, under his breath. "No way!"

Don sighed as if he had heard Steve's answer before. "If you want to leave home, there are several choices. You've talked about Alaska. That could be a satisfying adventure if you had a job there. Otherwise no way would I let you go up as a drifter. It's rougher than you could imagine, with too many others looking for work too. There's a good chance of getting a job on a seagoing ship. My friend Howie knows some of the crews on cargo freighters that come in here. You might be able to sign on a freighter as a deckhand and work your way wherever they're going—Australia, Indian Ocean, South Africa. And there are also commercial fishing boats in town that go up the Inland Passage to Alaska. Howie could probably get you a job on one of the fishing boats—low wages while you learn how to handle the boat and the fishing techniques. Another way to work with ships and the sea is the Coast Guard. I left some information about that on your dresser. I don't know what they would say about your arrest, but we could at least talk to them. So those are the choices so far, unless you come up with some others." He grinned at Steve as if the door was wide open. "So you figure out what you want to do, and tell me when you know, anytime before New Year's. Okay?"

Steve looked at him for a long moment and then smiled, an open smile that looked as if some strain had ended.

"I guess I can figure out something by that time," he said. He hesitated, swallowed, and added, "And—thanks, Don!"

The telephone rang, and Jennie got up to answer it.

"Oh, hi, Kim!" she said, glancing toward Steve. He was shaking his head and signaling no. "Steve? Let me see if I can find him."

She muffled the mouthpiece and looked at Steve again. He shook his head and said, "I can't talk to her right now. Maybe I'll see her tomorrow."

"Kim, Steve says he can't talk just now . . . No, nothing is wrong here. He's just kind of involved in something. He says maybe he'll see you tomorrow."

She hung up the telephone and said to Steve accusingly, "She said she hadn't seen you at school to talk to since last week. Are you breaking up or something?"

"Well, she's been pushing me to take that English course over again, and decide about going to college. I told her I didn't know what I was going to do next year, and now she's trying to make me make up my mind!" He shook his head somberly. "Girls! Sometimes I think you never satisfy them unless you do just what they tell you they want you to do." He looked at Jennie challengingly. "So whose business is it what I decide to do next year?"

He threw down his napkin and left the table.

"Gee, I thought he was over being mad," Tommy said.

"You can hardly blame a guy if he feels everybody is leaning on him so hard that he has no free air to fly in," Don said. "Now, nobody ask Steve anything about his plans. Just act as if he's doing everything right and don't talk about it . . . and don't ask about Kim, either."

16

Friday was the last day of school before Christmas vacation. Liza stood by her locker at the end of the afternoon, trying to decide what books she wanted to take home. The shelf was jammed with books and papers. She lifted the pile to the floor and knelt down to sort out notebooks, scrap papers, books that should go back to the library (she found one that was a week overdue), and get everything organized before she left it for two weeks.

As she began sorting, she heard Kim cry brightly, "Why, Steve! How are you?" and then, "Have you got a minute? I've been wanting to talk to you."

Liza glanced over her shoulder. Steve had an armload of books, and a bag filled with more books. Neither of them seemed to notice her.

"Why, Steve! What on earth? You look as if you're taking everything home!"

He lifted his chin in that independent manner Liza had liked when she first met him. "Yeah. I am."

"But aren't you coming back?"

He shrugged. "Probably not. What did you want to talk about?"

They moved a few feet away, into a window recess behind the corner of Liza's locker.

"I've been worried about you, Steve," Kim said plaintively. "Not seeing you at school or anything. Is something wrong?"

"Nothing special," Steve said, as if he didn't want to talk about it. "Why? I've been busy working with Don, mostly."

"Well, it was something I heard," Kim said very seriously. "I hate even to think about it. But one of the boys said you had to go to court Wednesday, when you weren't in school. Because of shoplifting!"

"So?" Steve sounded gruff. "It isn't the kind of thing you go around announcing!"

"But with the relationship we've had, I should think the least you could do was tell me about it. If you can't be honest with me, there's just nothing there—"

"It had nothing to do with our relationship!" Steve was impatient. "It's nobody else's business. It's just between Don and me now. And I don't want to talk about it."

"But, Steve, if you don't care what I think, and if I can't even know why you do something like that, how can we have any real understanding? How can I know you, really and honestly, if I don't know why you have to steal? You don't care what I think! You don't even care whether I understand or not!" She spoke so intensely that her voice shook.

Steve said stubbornly and angrily, "There're

135

some things I don't have to talk about, and that's just how it is. Everything was going along just fine last summer. Then you began telling me what I should be doing, and I don't take that kind of thing."

"But if you cared about me the way you used to, we could talk about things."

"Maybe it's changed." He sounded as if he was hardly sure how he felt and was exploring with words to find out. "Maybe I'm not going to finish this year. I might have other plans and not even come back after Christmas. I can't talk about things like that. I just have to figure them out by myself—and with no interference."

"But it's such a waste!" Kim wailed. "You could be so great! And if you're just going to be a dropout —Why, Steve? Why throw it all away like that?"

He stiffened angrily. "That's where you couldn't understand if I talked about it all night! I've got to find my own way, and if I fail, if I turn out to be a loser, it's going to be going my own way and not doing what someone else tells me to!"

She clutched her books and stared up at him, and her voice broke as she cried, "But, Steve! I thought—I really thought we had something going that was real and forever."

"That's what I thought once." He sounded tired. "But how can anyone tell? You wanted me to be honest, Kim. So here it is: I don't feel the way I did for a while. Not enough to say it's going to be forever. And I can't face any more of this school. Not now. Not after Christmas. Not ever. So I'm going to train for work with ships—go to sea—and I can't wait!"

136

There was a silence. Liza looked around the open door of her locker. Steve was staring stiffly out of the window, and Kim was wiping her eyes as if she resented the tears.

"Will I see you again?" she asked.

"I won't have much time from now on," Steve said. "I'm working with Don pretty steadily until I leave."

Then, as she buried her face in a handful of tissues, he patted her shoulder and said, "Kim, I'm sorry it had to break up this way. It was good while it lasted, but we're going in different directions now. And that's the way it's got to be."

She turned, blowing her nose, and rushed down the hall away from him. He watched her go, shaking his head. Then he turned and went out the nearest door to the bicycle rack, with his load of books and papers.

Liza put her own books and papers back on the shelf, slipped on her jacket, picked up a book and notebook to take home, and went out a different door.

She slid up on the counter stool in front of the ice-cream counter in Applegate's pharmacy on the last day of the year.

"Give me an ice-cream cone, Barney. Vanilla. Kind of small."

He scooped up the ice cream, kind of small as she had asked, pushed it into a sugar cone and handed it to her.

"How was Christmas at your house?"

"It was okay." She licked the cone thoughtfully. "This whole year has been so mixed up that sometimes I wondered if we'd have any Christmas at all. Did you hear about Steve?"

Barney nodded, wiping off the counter. Then he fixed a cone for himself and came around to sit on the stool next to Liza. It was one thirty, and the store was almost empty.

"I heard about his getting arrested. So what's he going to do now?"

"Well, he was released in Dad's custody, and Dad told him he'd have to shape up and decide what he's going to do from now on. If he stayed home, he was going to have to work with Dad and not see his friends and finish school." She licked her cone thoughtfully. "But Steve always wanted to go to sea. So he decided to enlist in the Coast Guard day before yesterday. And next week he reports to boot camp in California. And maybe he'll get to go to Alaska with the Coast Guard someday." She paused a moment and licked her cone again. "The Coast Guard wasn't all that keen about his not finishing high school. But they talked to him a long time and said they'd take a chance."

"I wouldn't mind the Coast Guard service," Barney said. "They've got some great boats, with those cutters and search-and-rescue ships, and the ice-breakers up in Prudhoe Bay—"

"I think he's going to like the service," Liza said. "Anyway, I hope he comes out different, because I don't like him much the way he is now."

"You always kind of liked him, didn't you?"

138

Liza nodded. "At first I thought he was great. And it's a terrible feeling when somebody lets you down like that. You wonder who you can count on." She looked at her watch and slid off the stool. "I've gotta run. Maggie wants me to help with some New Year's cooking. Here's the money for the cone."

"So it looks as if old Steve is going to come out all right," Barney said.

"Dad thinks he will." Liza slung her bag over her shoulder. "It's all shaping up better than I expected. I even like Jennie now."

She rode off toward home, reflecting on the end of the old year.

"Better than I expected," she said again. Aloud.

About the Author

ANNE EMERY is the author of many popular books, some based on the experiences and perspectives of her own five children. A teacher before her marriage, she has intense and many-faceted empathy for the problems and interests of young readers.

Mrs. Emery and her husband live on Orcas Island, Washington, where they retired after an active life in Evanston, Illinois.